The Maestro's Treasure

By
David Leadbeater

Copyright © 2024 by David Leadbeater
ISBN: 9798344412955

All rights reserved.
No part of this publication may be reproduced, distributed, or transmitted in any form or by any means, including photocopying, recording, or other electronic or mechanical methods, without the prior written permission of the publisher/author except in the case of brief quotations embodied in critical reviews and certain other non-commercial uses permitted by copyright law.
All characters in this book are fictitious, and any resemblance to actual persons living or dead is purely coincidental.

Classification: Thriller, adventure, action, mystery, suspense, archaeological, military, historical, assassination, terrorism, assassin, spy

Other Books by David Leadbeater:

Blood Requiem

The Matt Drake Series
A constantly evolving, action-packed romp based in the escapist action-adventure genre:

The Bones of Odin (Matt Drake #1)
The Blood King Conspiracy (Matt Drake #2)
The Gates of Hell (Matt Drake 3)
The Tomb of the Gods (Matt Drake #4)
Brothers in Arms (Matt Drake #5)
The Swords of Babylon (Matt Drake #6)
Blood Vengeance (Matt Drake #7)
Last Man Standing (Matt Drake #8)
The Plagues of Pandora (Matt Drake #9)
The Lost Kingdom (Matt Drake #10)
The Ghost Ships of Arizona (Matt Drake #11)
The Last Bazaar (Matt Drake #12)
The Edge of Armageddon (Matt Drake #13)
The Treasures of Saint Germain (Matt Drake #14)
Inca Kings (Matt Drake #15)
The Four Corners of the Earth (Matt Drake #16)
The Seven Seals of Egypt (Matt Drake #17)
Weapons of the Gods (Matt Drake #18)
The Blood King Legacy (Matt Drake #19)
Devil's Island (Matt Drake #20)
The Fabergé Heist (Matt Drake #21)
Four Sacred Treasures (Matt Drake #22)

The Sea Rats (Matt Drake #23)
Blood King Takedown (Matt Drake #24)
Devil's Junction (Matt Drake #25)
Voodoo soldiers (Matt Drake #26)
The Carnival of Curiosities (Matt Drake #27)
Theatre of War (Matt Drake #28)
Shattered Spear (Matt Drake #29)
Ghost Squadron (Matt Drake #30)
A Cold Day in Hell (Matt Drake #31)
The Winged Dagger (Matt Drake #32)
Two Minutes to Midnight (Matt Drake #33)
The Devil's Reaper (Matt Drake #34)
The Dark Tsar (Matt Drake #35)

The Alicia Myles Series
Aztec Gold (Alicia Myles #1)
Crusader's Gold (Alicia Myles #2)
Caribbean Gold (Alicia Myles #3)
Chasing Gold (Alicia Myles #4)
Galleon's Gold (Alicia Myles #5)
Hawaiian Gold (Alicia Myles #6)

The Torsten Dahl Thriller Series
Stand Your Ground (Dahl Thriller #1)

The Relic Hunters Series
The Relic Hunters (Relic Hunters #1)
The Atlantis Cipher (Relic Hunters #2)
The Amber Secret (Relic Hunters #3)
The Hostage Diamond (Relic Hunters #4)
The Rocks of Albion (Relic Hunters #5)

The Illuminati Sanctum (Relic Hunters #6)
The Illuminati Endgame (Relic Hunters #7)
The Atlantis Heist (Relic Hunters #8)
The City of a Thousand Ghosts (Relic Hunters #9)
Hierarchy of Madness (Relic Hunters #10)

The Joe Mason Series
The Vatican Secret (Joe Mason #1)
The Demon Code (Joe Mason #2)
The Midnight Conspiracy (Joe Mason #3)
The Babylon Plot (Joe Mason #4)
The Traitor's Gold (Joe Mason #5)
The Angel Deception (Joe Mason #6)

The Rogue Series
Rogue (Book One)

The Disavowed Series:
The Razor's Edge (Disavowed #1)
In Harm's Way (Disavowed #2)
Threat Level: Red (Disavowed #3)

The Chosen Few Series
Chosen (The Chosen Trilogy #1)
Guardians (The Chosen Trilogy #2)
Heroes (The Chosen Trilogy #3)

Short Stories
Walking with Ghosts (A short story)
A Whispering of Ghosts (A short story)

All genuine comments are very welcome at:

davidleadbeater2011@hotmail.co.uk

Twitter: @dleadbeater2011

Visit David's website for the latest news and information:
davidleadbeater.com

The Maestro's Treasure

CHAPTER ONE

The night was progressing well, Ricky thought, as he looked over at Bruce. His companion was currently hauling out piles of money from a recently opened safe. Ricky was busy helping himself to a lucky find, a jewellery collection that had been hidden in a drawer. Bruce started stuffing the piles of money into a large rucksack and then beckoned Ricky to throw his over.

'What you got there?' Bruce asked.

Ricky waved a diamond studded necklace. 'A little extra for our efforts.'

'Let's make it quick. We only have a twenty-minute window.'

Ricky nodded and stuffed his pocket with jewellery before zipping them up. Next, he went across the office to help Bruce load up. The office was quite small and square, populated with a desk, two chairs, and a giant safe. Ricky was at Bruce's side in moments. He crouched down, reached into the safe, and scooped out more cash.

'Too much to carry,' he said.

'A good problem.'

'I've had worse days,' Ricky grinned.

Together, the men filled their rucksacks almost to overflowing and then fastened them. Ricky took a surreptitious glance at the door. There was no immediate sound, only a faint roar of noise emanating through the floorboards from the boisterous casino above. The bosses of the underground casino spent all of their nights either on the gaming floor or ensconced in the luxurious offices above. Ricky and Bruce had done their homework well. They had done it so well it had taken them months of careful surveillance. Ricky had even got a job at the casino, working as a waiter. He knew the place inside out. Tonight was the culmination of a well-rehearsed plan.

Ricky rose to his feet and shrugged the now heavy rucksack over his shoulders. It was a good weight, he thought. Perfect. He looked once more towards the closed door.

'You think they suspect anything?'

Bruce looked surprised. 'You kidding? For them, tonight's just another night. They'll be sitting happily in their ivory towers watching people shovel in their hard earned cash to make them even richer. What we're doing, my friend, it's a service to all those who've ever lost in a gambling hall.'

Ricky laughed. 'We've done many similar services in our time.'

Bruce finished fastening his rucksack. 'That's why we're so damn good,' he said. 'Now, you ready?'

Ricky looked up at the ceiling. 'My least favourite part.'

Bruce closed the safe and climbed up onto the desk. 'Shouldn't eat so many burgers.'

'Screw you.'

Bruce fiddled with a ventilation grille, pulled it away from the wall. A wide passage was revealed.

Now all the men had to do was fit inside and crawl to another room where there was a window that led onto the fire escape. Bruce went first, sticking his head into the gap and looking around.

Ricky watched from below. 'Ha. Having trouble are-'

He never finished. Suddenly, the door flew open and smashed back against its hinges. A man rushed into the room, followed by three more and then another two. The room got very crowded. Ricky's mouth fell open, and he swallowed, his mouth now parched.

All the men except one carried guns or knives.

A tall man with a ponytail sauntered in at the back of the group. 'Well, well, what do we have here?' he said.

'Hey, hey, stay cool,' Bruce said, still on the desk.

'Caught red-handed,' the tall man said. 'With your fingers in the cookie jar. Let's chop them off, shall we?'

His men moved forward. Ricky, trying to hide his fear, backed up as much as he could. It wasn't far, and the rucksack now felt like a heavy anchor around his neck, weighing him down as he plunged through deep currents.

'Look, man,' he said, holding up both hands. 'Stay cool. We can talk about this.'

'Talk?' the tall man's eyes widened. 'Talk? Yes, you're gonna talk. I want to know how you did this, how you got so far, who hired you. I want it all.'

Bruce climbed gingerly off the desk and unhooked the rucksack. Ricky also removed his and held it out like an offering. 'It's all there,' he said weakly.

'Grab them,' the tall man said.

His men moved fast and with precision. They took the rucksacks and then grabbed hold of Ricky and Bruce. Both men were thrust into chairs and positioned in front of the desk. The tall man stood before them.

'My name is Leo, but you probably already know that, don't you? I also assume you know who I am. I run four of these rather pleasant dens of iniquity across the city. It's a good job, and I intend to keep it. Now, getting robbed would have severely affected the good light in which I'm seen by my bosses. Do you understand?'

Both Ricky and Bruce nodded. Ricky's eyes were enormous, the fear building endlessly in his chest. Where the hell had they gone wrong? Leo had an evil reputation, and now they were at his mercy.

'What can we do to make amends?' he asked.

Leo smiled as he said, 'How about a couple of fingers to start with? Let's see how that goes.'

He gestured to his men. They grabbed Ricky and Bruce by their arms, spread their fingers on the desk. Ricky bit his bottom lip so hard it started bleeding. He could only watch as the knife dipped towards his little finger.

And then came the pain. Ricky couldn't hold it in. He screamed as he watched his finger severed and blood pool across the desk. Next to him, Bruce did the same.

'Ah, the sounds of justice,' Leo said, still smiling. 'The music of agony. Now, look at those bags full of my money and ask yourselves – did I do the right thing?'

Ricky licked blood from around his lips as he

stared at his finger, now lying gruesomely on the desk. He couldn't believe they'd been caught, that the tables had been turned so quickly. Minutes ago, he was buoyed up, shooting the shit with his friend about another successful job. Now...he dreaded what was to come.

'Who hired you?' Leo asked.

Bruce answered quickly. 'We're working solo,' he said. 'Side job.'

Leo shook his head. 'Another finger,' he said. 'Just him for now,' then he turned to Ricky. 'Same question.'

Ricky kept his bloody lips closed tight. He couldn't tell them they worked for the Diablos. It would start a gang war. Instead, he gritted his teeth and then screamed as they took another finger.

Leo watched contentedly. 'We have all night, boys,' he said. 'We're just getting started,' he looked at his men. 'Are you guys having as much fun as I am?'

Ricky tried to close his mind to the pain and the gory sights as Leo's men continued to hack and chop at him. There was a lot of blood. Leo seemed to delight in it. The men never went near their guns; they were content to use their knives and cudgels. They cut and sliced and crushed until Ricky's head was lost in pain, until he'd forgotten who he was and why he was here. The only thing he felt and saw was a haze of red.

'You're gonna tell me everything I want to know,' was all he heard. Leo's calm, even tones. The man never changed his manner, even as the room filled with the scent of murder. His men went about their tasks efficiently and mundanely, as if they'd done it a hundred times. And they probably had.

There was a time when both men broke, when they stopped recalling reality and just spouted what Leo wanted to hear. Somewhere in the back of his mind, Ricky knew he had broken, that it had always been inevitable, and he could have saved himself a lot of pain by just coming clean straight away. But that wasn't the way it was done. He was loyal to the Diablos, and Leo was going to kill him anyway.

Both him and Bruce.

They had had a good run. They'd started working for the Diablos decades ago and had pulled countless jobs, most of them successful. Their wins had made them a big part of the gang, an essential cog.

But one small failure had cost them their lives. What went wrong? Ricky knew vaguely that he would never know. He also knew that he faced death, that he would never see the sun again, never breathe fresh air. He had fainted twice, but they kept bringing him around, kept him awake and aware of everything that was happening.

Close to the end, Leo leaned in and slapped both their faces to make them more conscious. 'You made a mistake when you stole from me, and so did the Diablos. I really don't appreciate it, as you can probably tell. Well...I think we've got all we're gonna get from you. I wonder what happens next.'

Ricky was vaguely aware of a knife resting against his chest, over his heart. He looked down, saw it glinting bloodily. He was so far gone he didn't feel any extra fear, any regret, anything at all.

He just felt numb.

The blade ripped into him, and finally Ricky felt no pain.

CHAPTER TWO

Guy Bodie was a happy man. About a month had passed since they escaped the terrifying ordeal of the contest and they'd all recovered nicely. Bodie and Heidi had picked up where they had left off before they were abducted. Bodie enjoyed that – because they had been dating. It had taken them a long time to get that far, but the wait had been worth it.

Right now, they were in a movie theatre, watching some action flick that he wasn't bothered about. He was more interested in the woman beside him, and was waiting for the movie to end so they could get closer. She smiled at him now, her eyes crinkling. He smiled back at the knowledge their relationship was in a good place.

When the movie ended, they left the theatre and stepped into some typical cooling New York drizzle. Heidi grabbed his hand and swung it up and down, walking quickly.

'You don't wanna grab a cab?' Bodie asked.

'It's just a few blocks. The rain's nice.'

'Ya think? It'll mess up my hair.' He had very little.

'Well, I don't care because mine's already a mess.' She ran a hand through her frizzy hair. 'Can't do a thing with it. Never have been able to.'

Bodie kept walking, unsure whether he should disagree or just keep quiet. He chose the latter. To be fair, the rain wasn't too bad and by the time they'd reached Heidi's apartment he was barely wet.

Heidi unlocked the door, and he followed her up a set of stairs to her room. They had each rented their own places now since the reward money finally came through and were enjoying a few well-earned months off. What was going to happen after that, or what direction they were going to take, nobody knew. But, as a group, they'd been through a lot together during the last few years and wanted a little time off before any serious discussions got started.

Heidi went into the kitchen and poured two glasses of red wine. She offered one to Bodie, who took it and sipped. He took his jacket off and went over to her.

'It's been a good night,' he said.

'It's about to get better.'

He looked around. 'Why? Do you have *Shrek* on rental?'

She laughed and put a hand on his arm. 'No. I have another guy coming over.'

This time Bodie laughed. They embraced. Heidi sipped her drink over his shoulder. The furthering of their relationship had been a long time coming, but Bodie was intensely happy that they had now come this far.

It had always been the natural progression. Ever since they met in Mexico, Bodie had felt something between them, some kind of attraction. Finally, it had come to fruition.

'Are you happy?' Heidi asked him suddenly.

He blinked. 'Are you kidding? I'm right where I want to be, having the best time of my life.'

'You sure?'

'Of course, I'm sure. Why do you ask?'

'Just my insecurity, I guess. I don't do well with relationships. And you...well you're used to gallivanting, adventuring, globetrotting...'

'Relic hunting.'

'Yeah, all of that. You don't seem the kind of guy who settles down.'

'You make me sound like an action hero.'

They both laughed and embraced again. The drinks were emptied and then Heidi brought her lips up to his. Soon, they were lost in each other as the rain spattered against the windows and the night grew darker still.

Nothing else mattered.

Reilly sat opposite Yasmine at the far end of a high-end eating establishment on Broadway. The place was filled with quiet merriment, the other diners enjoying their meals and company. Reilly and Yasmine had decided to go out together to relive some of their old adventures and fun times.

'There's nothing like a night of reminiscing,' Reilly said. 'How long is it since we were together?'

Yasmine shook her head, her shiny long black hair brushing her shoulders. 'I haven't kept track. But I remember you being a bad boy back then.'

Reilly hung his head a little. 'I got caught up in all that,' he said. 'Didn't want to do it. But when you're in a gang, it's hard to get out. To break free with no comebacks. As you know, I had to run away to the Amazon in the end.'

'But it did get you free.'

Reilly shrugged. 'I just hope they've stopped looking for me.'

'It'd be some serious bad luck if they found you now.'

'It happens.'

'We're just getting on our feet,' Yasmine said. 'The reward money finally came through. We aren't in any immediate danger.' She smiled, spearing a chunk of steak. 'And we all survived our contests without too much psychological damage. At least, as far as I can tell.'

Reilly nodded. 'I was wondering what the hell we were going to do before the reward money came through. I thought we were out on the streets for a while. Thank God we found that treasure in that mine, although doing so almost killed us.'

'Been there a few times whilst working with Bodie,' Yasmine said. 'Danger seems attracted to him. Just like you.'

'You think I'm a danger magnet? Do you feel safe with me?' He half smiled.

'Around you, anything could happen.' She gave him a grin. 'Have you had any thoughts about what you want to do next?'

'I guess that depends if Bodie's gonna keep up with the relic hunting.'

'You want to stay with the team?'

He took a sip of wine. 'Do you?'

'I've become a permanent fixture, yeah. I want the team to keep going. We have an excellent reputation. Unfortunately, a lot of what we found wasn't made public because we were working for the CIA, but still...the right people know. Maybe they could offer us a few jobs.'

'A way to get started,' Reilly nodded. 'Maybe I will stay with the team, if they'll have me.'

'After what you did to help in the last mission, I'm sure they will. You helped save everyone's life.'

Reilly looked down, a smile stretching across his face. 'I did my best.'

'If the team continues, I'll be staying,' Yasmine told him. 'Maybe you should think about doing so too.'

'You don't mind me being around?'

She shrugged. 'We have a history. So what? It's as ancient as some of those relics we've found. I'm okay with it if you are.'

Reilly nodded. 'Oh, I'm fine. I'm also fine taking it easy for a while. Do you know something? Until now, I've never stopped.'

She frowned. 'Never stopped?'

'Moving. Running. Chasing. I don't remember the last time I took a proper break, if ever.'

Yasmine stared at him thoughtfully. 'I feel something similar,' she said. 'What a pair we make.'

'Any idea what's next on the agenda?'

'Bodie will call us all together eventually. I think the decision has to be unanimous. There's Jemma and Lucie and Cassidy to think of. There's Heidi. I think Bodie will want everyone on the same page to reach a decision.'

'And in the meantime...let's enjoy ourselves.'

They sat contentedly in the restaurant, enjoying their meals, surrounded by frivolity and laughter. The rain beat constantly at the windows, but it didn't dampen the atmosphere. The serving staff came and went and did their jobs well. Bar staff brought drinks that tasted superb; both of them were on cocktails. It was a fun night catching up, and neither of them had any idea what was just around the corner.

'Here's to the future,' Reilly raised his colourful drink.

'For once, I'm looking forward to it.'

'Let's hope the others are, too. Where are they tonight, anyway?'

'Bodie and Heidi are on a date. Cassidy took Jemma and Lucie on a night out.'

Reilly winced. 'That sounds dangerous.'

'For New York?' Yasmine said. 'It probably is.'

CHAPTER THREE

Cassidy put down her drink and rose to her feet. The music was booming. Across from her, Jemma and Lucie looked up expectantly.

'Another round?' Lucie asked.

Cassidy swayed, felt the world move around her, and sat back down. She'd been sinking twice as much as the other two tonight, and the effects were starting to take their toll. It probably wasn't a good idea to drink any more.

'Dance?' Jemma said.

Cassidy felt decidedly sick at the thought. 'I think I'll pass. I need to sober up a bit. But you guys feel free.'

They were seated in the quietest corner of the club, but even that was noisy. There were tables all around them, a dancefloor just ten or twelve metres away and a loudspeaker to the right of their heads. Dance tracks filled the air, and the floor was crowded with writhing men and women.

'Thanks for coming out with me tonight,' Cassidy said, leaning forward.

Lucie, despite the drink, still looked uneasy. Of all of them, she was the introvert. 'It's all a bit too *peopley* for me.'

'Yeah, I get it,' Cassidy said. 'You historians are used to dusty books and ancient passageways.'

'I miss that life,' Lucie said wistfully.

Cassidy stared at her. 'You can forget your problems in a place like this.'

Lucie shrugged. 'Likewise in an ancient passageway.'

Jemma decided she was getting another round of drinks and headed off to the bar. Cassidy ordered a diet Pepsi, determined to avoid alcohol for the rest of the night. Maybe she should get them all up to dance. They'd already hit the floor three times tonight, and had been hit upon every single time. They shrugged the attentions off. They weren't in the mood for more company tonight, male or female.

Jemma eventually returned, balancing the three drinks precariously. She set them on the table and retook her seat. This was the first time they had really let their hair down for as long as they could remember and was probably one reason Cassidy had slightly overdone it. But, she thought, the night was still young.

'Are you staying with the team?' Jemma asked suddenly.

Cassidy blinked. 'Am I...of course! I've been with Bodie for over ten years. What the hell else would I do? Write books?' She laughed.

'You probably have a few good adventures stories in you,' Jemma grinned.

'That'd be an autobiography,' Cassidy said. 'I've been an actress. A fighter. I've lived on the street. And, oh, I found quite a few dusty old relics. You think I could market that?'

'Wouldn't hurt to try,' Lucie said with a serious shrug.

Cassidy turned to Jemma. 'What about you?' She said. 'You've been with Bodie almost as long as I have. Do you have any plans for moving on?'

'Well, I'm not getting any younger,' Jemma sat back. 'And all the rushing around is starting to tell on the old bones. But it beats getting a gym membership.' She smiled to show she was joking. 'I don't like the danger, but the life is good.'

'And what about you, Lucie?' Cassidy asked.

Lucie still looked serious. 'I don't like how we've been targeted,' she said. 'By certain individuals. But I also like the life. Hunting relics is what I do. I'm looking forward to the next one.'

'Then you think we should form an agency? Specifically dedicated to hunting relics. Offer ourselves out for work?'

'Yeah, I do. We have the right skill sets. We have the contacts. The personnel. I think we're set up to succeed at it.'

'This definitely needs a larger conversation,' Cassidy said. 'With Bodie involved. And the others. And I think it should come soon. We...we were lucky during the last mission, and we all learned something about ourselves.'

'We learned how to survive against the odds,' Lucie said, suppressing a shudder. During the last mission, where they had been abducted, they had been forced to endure various contests against differing opponents and, to live or die, they had been forced to win. Lucie still refused to talk deeply about her own ordeal.

'It's better out in the open,' Jemma said pointedly to her.

'Not here. Not tonight. Not any night. I can't do it.'

Cassidy lifted her drink, trying to throw off the sudden discontent. 'Let's continue the party,' she said. 'No negativity tonight.'

'How about…to the future?' Jemma raised her own drink.

'I like the sound of that so long as it's as part of the team,' Cassidy said. 'For me, it's forever.'

Jemma clinked glasses. 'Me too.'

Lucie tried to wipe the serious look off her face and gave them a smile. 'I'm all for it,' she responded. 'Like I said, this is me for life.'

The trio drank a little, talked a lot, and then, as time passed, visited the dance floor again. The lights spun, and the music flowed, and they lost all sense of reality for a while. There were no burdens, no worries, no apprehension about tomorrow. It wasn't the drink that did it ultimately; it was the company.

It was a good night, and it was exactly what they needed. Soon, decisions would be required. But, for now, they were far away. Or so it seemed.

CHAPTER FOUR

Reilly and Yasmine sat chilling in a quiet corner of an old pub. The night was getting older now; the establishment emptying out, the old timers lining the bar and a few couples occupying the tables. Reilly drank in the quiet, savouring it. Next to him, Yasmine seemed content. Just like old friends, they didn't have to talk to enjoy their evening. Companionship was enough.

Yasmine finally spoke after a long silence. 'I wonder if the others are on the same page? About staying and working together?'

Reilly sipped his pint. 'I'm fresh blood,' he said. 'I don't have a say, really. But I'd be up for it.'

'Of course you have a say,' Yasmine frowned. 'You've proved yourself a valuable team member. I'd vouch for you, for your vote.'

'Thanks,' he nodded. 'I'd like to join the famous relic hunting team.'

'Famous?'

'Cassidy says you're famous, so I must agree.'

'Good point. I-'

Right then, Reilly's phone started to ring. He looked surprised, then fished the device out of his pocket. 'Who the hell could that be?'

'One way to find out,' Yasmine said.

Reilly looked at the screen. 'Unknown caller,' he said. 'Probably trying to sell me condoms.'

He pushed the green button and answered the call. 'Hello?'

'Is that Reilly?' A brusque voice asked.

'Who is this?'

'Remy Green. Is that Reilly?'

'How the hell did you get this number?'

'I have the same contacts as you, man, and they know how desperate I am to get hold of you.'

Reilly felt his entire body go cold. Remy Green was a true blast from the past. When Reilly had worked for the Diablos, Remy had been his next in command, kind of a lieutenant. Remy had taken a shine to Reilly and always looked out for him, given him the cushier jobs. It was because of Remy that Reilly worked the non-violent jobs and got involved in less criminality. Throughout his time in the Diablos, Remy had been there to look out for him. In fact, the only misgivings Reilly had about escaping their clutches centred around Remy. The man had invested a lot of time and effort into him, shielded him beyond expectation.

'Remy,' he said. 'I...I don't know what to say.'

'It's been a while, and you left me in the shit. Well and truly in the shit. I vouched for you and it almost got me killed. But a lot of water's passed under the bridge since then. That's all in the past. And shit, I'm still looking out for you.'

Reilly's body temperature hadn't risen any, and now he felt something dark grip his soul. 'What the hell are you talking about?' He could have said a hundred things. Could have said he was untouchable, out of the game, working for a competitor, on the other side of the world, or that he didn't care, but Reilly had a deep respect for Remy and instinctually knew his best interests were now at heart.

'Listen, are you sitting down? You really need to for this, man. I don't know a way out.'

Reilly licked dry lips. 'Go on.'

'All right, man. All right. Do you remember Ricky and Bruce?'

Reilly had another flashback. Ricky and Bruce always came as a double act, and they were a formidable team. Two of the best in the game, but not to Reilly's liking. They had a penchant for unnecessary violence. Unfortunately, two or three times, Reilly had been forced to work with them.

'I remember those bastards,' he said shortly. 'What are they up to now?'

'Well, not a whole lot. They're dead. Bodies found a few days ago.'

Reilly wasn't upset, nor was he surprised. 'They lived hard and probably died hard.'

'They certainly did.'

'So what do their deaths have to do with me?'

'A whole lot, unfortunately. Do you recall the Gustave Auch heist?'

Reilly felt a jolt in his heart. Suddenly, this all started to make sense. 'Oh, no,' he said involuntarily.

'You do. It was Ricky, Bruce, and you who did the job. Do you remember the details?'

Reilly didn't have to trawl his memories. It was probably the biggest job of his criminal career. He kept his voice low. 'We stole thirteen paintings. It was one of the gang's best ever nights. Out of the thirteen, four were Rembrandts. It was a fair few years ago. We stashed the art until the heat wore off, but the heat never wore off. We found out later that the heist was worth 500 million. We stashed them in storage until a later date.'

'And now do you get it?'

'Oh yeah. Ricky, Bruce and me are the only three people on earth who know where the stolen art went.'

'And now both Ricky and Bruce are dead.'

'So where does that leave me?'

Remy drew a deep breath. 'Do you really have to ask?'

Reilly needed to know the full picture. 'Do the gang want their art back?'

'The murders of Ricky and Bruce have highlighted the fact that one of their old jobs was basically unfinished. The art is still there, lost. The Diablos want it back.'

'And the heat might have worn off by now.'

'Well, it's cooled, that's for sure. Reilly – the Diablos are actively, purposely, looking for you.'

'I don't want their damn art. Maybe I could send them an anonymous tip.'

Remy snorted. 'You don't send anonymous tips to the fucking Diablos. They go out and get what they want.'

Reilly had known it. 'Is there not a way to go through you?'

'I understand why you might say that. But my standing isn't as good with the new younger bosses these days. They don't listen like they used to. It's all rushing into things and diving headlong instead of taking a step back and listening. They've got themselves into some real trouble but, hey, that's who they are these days, man.'

'So you're saying there's nothing I can do? That they're hunting for me, and they're gonna find me?'

'That's the reason for the heads up. The Diablos are big, well connected. If you're near any major and some minor cities, they'll have the means to find you. They're already on it. You have to lie low for...umm...for-'

'The rest of my life?'

'Maybe they'll get bored with looking in a month or two.'

'With 500 million up for grabs, I doubt it.'

'Reilly, we go way back. I just wanted you to know, to stay safe. If I can find you, they can.'

'How long did it take you?'

'A couple of weeks.'

'Shit, they could be on to me already.' He was staring at Yasmine, but then his eyes flitted around the pub, searching. He couldn't help it. Already, he was on edge.

'What's the way out of this?' he said. 'What can I do, Remy?'

'Be a ghost, man. Be a ghost.'

Remy ended the call with a sigh and an apology. Yasmine was sitting on the edge of her seat. Reilly knew she'd overheard his side of the conversation and quickly filled her in on the rest. He glanced anxiously around the pub.

'We should go.'

'If they knew you were here, they'd be on you already.'

'I know. But I need time to think.'

Yasmine put a hand on his, pinning it to the

table. 'There is a way out of this. You're just not thinking properly.'

Reilly narrowed his eyes at her. 'You have an idea?'

'Of course. Your team.'

'What do you mean?'

'I mean, we need to talk. All of us. Let's get the team together and discuss. You know our experience. We'll come up with something...something special, I promise.'

'The Diablos are extremely dangerous,' Reilly said. 'It'd be like putting the team in boiling water.'

'We can handle that. We've handled all sorts. But weren't you supposed to be part of the mafia at some point?'

Reilly shrugged. 'The Diablos have associations with the mafia. We were often loaned out. It only makes them more dangerous.'

'Then let's get the team together,' Yasmine said. 'Together, we'll make it work.'

Reilly felt the slightest sensation of hope. If anyone could help him get out of this, it was the relic hunters.

'All right,' he said. 'Make the call.'

CHAPTER FIVE

It was the next morning and the entire team had decided to meet in Heidi's apartment. Bodie was already there, and by nine a.m. everyone else had assembled. They all stood around the kitchen area, resting on the countertop and the breakfast bar or perching on stools. Bodie had a steaming cup of black coffee in front of him.

'Tell us everything,' he said. 'Right from the beginning.'

Reilly went over everything he'd discussed with Remy the night before. In particular, the details of the thirteen painting heist and its worth. He also mentioned Ricky and Bruce and how they had brought even more unnecessary heat to the job by killing two guards. The murders were avoidable, and they had made Reilly sick to the stomach. It was the last time he ever took a job with Ricky and Bruce.

'We've all done things we regret in the past,' Bodie said, referring to their own criminal activities a long time ago where they had robbed only from those who could afford it. 'We can't change that. But we can go forward better.'

'That's what I've been doing,' Reilly said. 'I hid out as best I could. I thought the gang had forgotten me. Now...it's all back full force.'

Bodie drank coffee, mind working. 'What can you tell us about the heist? The paintings?'

'Only that there were thirteen of them, including four Rembrandts. I remember there was some controversy over which paintings were the most valuable. Obviously, you'd go immediately to the Rembrandts, but there was something about the other nine. Some ancient mystery surrounding them.'

'Ancient mystery? You got anything clearer than that?'

'Not really. I just wanted to get in, get the art, and get out.'

Lucie was frowning. 'I can't recall anything about nine paintings and an ancient mystery. Maybe it's something I could research.'

'Not the issue,' Bodie said. 'The problem is the Diablos and their search for Reilly. How bad are this gang?'

Reilly hung his head. 'They're up there with the worst of them. And that was years ago. Apparently, they're being run by younger, fresher blood now. People more inclined toward violence and risk taking. That's what Remy said, anyway.'

'So how do we keep Reilly hidden from the Diablos?' Heidi put it all in a nutshell.

'We move him back to the Amazon,' Yasmine said with a smile to show she was joking.

Reilly raised an eyebrow. 'That's actually not a bad idea.'

'I'm not moving to the Amazon,' Jemma said with a shiver. 'Too humid.'

'I don't think it's possible,' Heidi cut to the chase, speaking in a quiet voice. 'I think the Diablos will find him eventually. It's just a matter of time.'

'There are 8.8 million people in this city,' Yasmine said. 'Surely it won't be that easy.'

'Maybe not,' Bodie said. 'But do you really wanna take that chance?' He looked at Reilly. 'Do you?'

Reilly shook his head. 'It'd be risky. One sighting is all they need. And then...' he shuddered. 'They'd go to work on me.'

Lucie bit her top lip. 'We need to think outside the box.'

'I have an idea,' Bodie said.

All eyes turned to him.

'There is another way,' he continued. 'We go get the treasure ourselves.'

The others looked at him. Heidi blinked. 'To what purpose?'

'We hand it back to the authorities. Maybe anonymously, I don't know yet. But if we reveal where it is, we negate the Diablos' purpose.'

Reilly was staring at him. 'And they don't need me anymore.'

'In that case,' Jemma said. 'Why do we have to go get it? Can't Reilly just tip the local police with the address?'

'No, no,' Reilly shook his head. 'I have to make sure it's there first. All intact as we left it. To be honest, it won't be too bad a trip.'

'But it will be dangerous,' Bodie said. 'After all, we're talking about investigating a criminal gang's 500 million dollar haul. Did you leave any fail safes behind?'

'A few cameras,' Reilly said. 'Motion detectors, all wired locally. Honestly, the gang wasn't interested because of the heat. They didn't want the attention such a massive haul would bring. The Gustave Auch treasure was huge. We didn't even realise until we'd done the job,' he shrugged. 'Is that good planning? Or bad planning?'

'It's put you in a world of shit,' Bodie said. 'So I'd lean towards the latter.'

'Where did you stash it?' Yasmine asked.

Reilly made a face. 'A fair but easy enough journey,' he said. 'It's in the Czech Republic.'

'You're kidding,' Bodie didn't look happy.

'Well, it was a van drive from the mark's home. It was the easiest place to put it. When you're on a job like this, you don't want unnecessary risk. You will decrease the danger if you can. That's all part of being a good criminal.' He shrugged.

Bodie looked like he didn't want to reflect on the past. 'I guess.'

'So we're headed to the Czech Republic?' Lucie said. 'To check on this haul and then inform the authorities. Get the bad guys off Reilly's back.'

'It seems like the best idea,' Jemma said. 'We can be there and back in a few days. And hopefully no one will recognise Reilly at the airport.'

'That's a chance we'll have to take,' Bodie said.

Lucie whipped out her laptop, already searching for flights. 'Shouldn't be too hard,' she said.

Bodie finished his coffee and went over to pour another. Cassidy had been standing by the window, keeping an eye on the street, and now sauntered over. 'I think we're pretty safe for now,' she said. 'I've not noticed anything suspect in the last week or so and I always keep an eye out.'

'Me too, to be fair,' Bodie said. 'My shit-o-meter is always on.'

Lucie looked at them both as if they were aliens. 'You never switch off? What about last night when you were pissed?'

Cassidy smiled a little. 'Like Guy said. The shit-o-meter is always on. You can never be too careful, especially in our line of work. I mean, look at what's happened recently with the abductions.'

'Did your shit-o-meter have a day off then?' Jemma asked.

'Oh, it worked all right. They were overwhelming odds, as you well know.'

Lucie was already booking flights. 'Right, so it's carry on and it leaves in about six hours. I suggest you pack light and fast. We'll meet back here to grab a cab.'

Reilly stood up first, casting a glance at them all. 'Thanks for doing this,' he said. 'For helping me.'

'We're a team,' Bodie said. 'Wouldn't have it any other way.'

The team all rose, grabbed their belongings, and walked purposefully out of the apartment. They didn't have long.

The Czech Republic beckoned.

CHAPTER SIX

The flight time to Prague was just under ten hours, so Bodie made the best of it. Since he and Heidi had been busy for much of the night, he hadn't got a lot of sleep and had been planning a lazy day. That had now changed, and they were on another mission. At least this one wasn't coerced, as the last had been.

Bodie sipped a few drinks, ate the food, and then tried to get some sleep. Usually, it worked. He could grab a nap anywhere. But here, today, he couldn't drop off. His mind kept going to Heidi, and running through what they were currently sharing. Yes, it had certainly been a long time coming, but it was all worth it now. He was loving life, and couldn't help but think this mission had come along at a rather inappropriate time. He wanted his time with Heidi to go on and on.

The plane bumped through some turbulence, further unsettling him. To his right, Heidi had her head back, doing exactly what he should be doing. The others were also napping, at ease during the flight. Bodie stared at his seat back, thinking.

These last few years had been a hell of a ride. They had worked for the CIA, found incredible treasures thought lost to history. They had even found Atlantis. The team had made a name for itself, but what did the future hold?

That was the second thing on Bodie's mind. They had money now, enough for a few years at least. Of course, it wouldn't last forever, so they couldn't retire even if they wanted to. But what was the next step? He knew without thinking that both Cassidy and Jemma would want to stay together. They had been a team for more than a decade. He knew also that turning themselves into a private relic hunting team was probably a good idea. They had the reputation and the connections to make it work. And, to be fair, he liked the idea. The only thing he didn't like was the danger.

They had already lost people along the way.

Bodie spent a few minutes remembering his old friends – people like Eli Cross and Sam Gunn – and then stored their memories away.

The journey went on, and soon he'd had enough to drink and too much to eat and he was bored again. His friends woke from their slumbers and started up a little conversation. Then, the plane was descending before bouncing gently across the tarmac.

Bodie was relieved. He didn't like inactivity, and there was nothing like being cooped up on a long journey, barely even able to leave your seat for more than a few minutes. He stood in line at border control and then they were free, walking through the airport to the car rental place.

Heidi was at his side.

'Sleep well?' He asked.

'Not really. I dreamed of you.'

He widened his eyes. 'Isn't that a good thing?'

'Believe me, it wasn't restful.'

He got the idea and grinned. They ended up

renting two cars so they could fit everyone in and walked out to the parking garage. Soon they were fiddling with sat navs and, finally, Bodie, in the lead car, turned to Reilly.

'Take us to your treasure haul, mate.'

It was around eight o'clock in the morning, local time. Bodie was worn-out, but didn't want to waste time resting. If they could get in and out of this place in just a few hours, it would be worth the fatigue.

Reilly directed them to a warehouse district and sat back. In this car, Cassidy was driving and negotiated the thick traffic with relative ease. It was a sunny day already, the skies blue and cloudless, and Bodie flicked the AC on. The sat nav told him they'd be at their destination in about ninety minutes, so he sat back, closed his eyes, and tried to drift.

Again, he wasn't successful. He wondered if he should broach the subject of their future to all those in the car, but decided it wasn't fair right now. Everyone needed to be involved and have an equal say.

Time eased by. Soon Cassidy was slowing. Yasmine, driving the follow car, stayed close. They entered the warehouse district Reilly had indicated and started negotiating the roads. It was a bleak area, industrial, sparse. Bodie saw long, low buildings with roller doors and shutters and barred windows. He looked back at Reilly, who sat in the back seat.

'You remember which one it was? They all look the bloody same to me.'

'Oh, I remember. It's the crappiest of them all.

Just keep heading towards the back of the estate.'

Cassidy did so, following his directions. Eventually, they ended up sitting at the kerb, staring at their destination.

Bodie wasn't impressed. The warehouse was a one-storey dark brick and block affair with a flat roof. It looked shabby, dirty, run down. Some windows were cracked. There was a sign up outside, forbidding any kind of entry. The pathways were overgrown with weeds, the concrete cracked and ragged. It looked like no one had been near it in years, which, Bodie thought, was probably the general idea.

'So what next?' Cassidy asked.

Bodie turned his attention to their surroundings. How busy was this area? He saw a tyre depot off to the right, doors wide open, with at least six cars on the ramps. He saw mechanics walking back and forth. A member of the public sat outside, waiting on a deck chair. Beyond that, there stood a sandwich shop and a builder's merchant. All were busy.

'It's not good,' he said. 'We need to use our skills to break into this place, not surveil it. Even the cars stand out like sore thumbs.'

There was no cover. No car parks. No fields of high hedges they could hide behind or use to approach the warehouse. Bodie waited until Lucie had taken some photos of the place and its surroundings and then asked Cassidy to find a parking area.

'It's definitely an after dark job,' Bodie said as they all gathered around the cars. 'We'll need supplies and appropriate clothing.'

'How do we get inside?' All eyes turned to Reilly.

'There is a keypad and a code. It's an easy one, don't worry.'

The rest of the day was spent visiting shops and pulling together their requirements. They rented rooms in a nearby hotel so they could stash the cars and get changed and then waited for full dark. When the time arrived, they set off separately, planning to meet by the warehouse.

Bodie slipped between buildings. He waited a while in a pool of shadows, checking to see if there was any security on the estate. They'd had a good drive round earlier and hadn't noticed any, but that might change after dark. Some time passed. He saw nothing except Cassidy's surreptitious shadow passing him by. He hugged the building, slipped around a corner and ran to the next. With the wide roads between buildings it was impossible to stay entirely hidden, but the team did its best.

Bodie eventually faced the warehouse they needed. It was wreathed in shadow. The dark sky above was cloudless, populated by stars, and a faint breeze blew past his face. In the distance, he could hear passing cars on a main road. There was nothing closer. He could smell rot and earth and something like old rubbish. He crouched in stillness for a while.

Saw Heidi and then Reilly make their way across the street. Nothing happened. All good so far. All they were here for was to check out the haul. Once they'd done that and determined it was all good, they could go home and inform the authorities. Once the news came out, the Diablos would back off.

At least, that was the hope.

Bodie made his own way across the street, easily finding the shadows and blending with them. He hadn't forgotten his old life, his old skills. He waited alongside Reilly as the others all made their way to the warehouse. Deep silence shrouded them. They didn't speak, but worked together, the essence of a great team. Reilly now led them around the side of the building to a door. Bodie saw nothing but fields in front of them and a waving straggly hedge. They were well hidden here.

'Do your work,' he whispered.

Reilly went to the door, found the keypad, and took a deep breath. 'It's been years,' he mumbled. 'Hope the code still works.'

'No reason it shouldn't,' Cassidy said.

Reilly input the code. The keypad's grimy light turned from red to green. Reilly heaved a sigh of relief and pushed the door inwards. Bodie broke out the flashlights.

There was a sudden noise. The sound of a car passing. They all held their breaths and didn't move. The rumble of the engine got closer and then died. Someone had parked up close by. Bodie swore silently and then moved to the side of the building. He peeked around and saw a white coupe with two people sitting in the front seat. Seconds later, they both moved to the back. As Bodie watched, their arms went to the windows, and he saw a pair of legs raised in the air. He smiled grimly. It was clear what was happening in the car and it looked like the couple were fully focused on each other.

He returned to the team. 'We're good,' he said. 'But keep it to whispers. Someone *is* out there.'

'Security?' Jemma asked.

'Not really. Just a couple checking out each other's bodies.'

There were brief smiles and the nodding of heads. Reilly was poised by the door. Bodie raised his flashlight and nodded. 'Go ahead.'

Reilly led the way in. Bodie found himself in a cavernous space, the warehouse appearing larger because of one obvious thing.

It was empty.

Reilly started towards the far end. 'Don't worry,' he said. 'We stashed the haul along the back wall. Drove the truck right inside. You won't need the flashlights yet.'

He was right. The windows admitted some light from the starry sky, stark silver that washed the dusty floor. Bodie could see bulky shadows along the walls, as if something ungainly had been wrapped in sheets and stored there. A light dust floated in the air and the only sound was their hushed footsteps.

Reilly approached the far wall as their eyes became properly adjusted to the gloom. Bodie was a few steps behind him. He saw Reilly stop, saw his arms flap at his sides, and then watched as the man turned towards them all.

'Oh, my god,' he said. 'The paintings are gone.'

'What?' Lucie stared.

'But it's not possible. Nobody else knew. The Diablos were everything to Ricky and Bruce. They wouldn't have messed with anything. And I know I didn't. So...where...? How?' Reilly looked flabbergasted. 'It's not possible.'

CHAPTER SEVEN

Bodie stared at the place where the paintings should be. In their place sat a pile of old dusty sheets. 'They were under those?'

'Yeah, we wrapped them up tight. Took our time, did it properly. Someone has been here and taken them.'

'Shit.'

'You could say that. What the hell am I gonna do? The Diablos will never accept that I can't *find* the paintings because they've been stolen by someone else.'

Bodie nodded. 'You're right. The gang won't believe you. And even if they did, they'd still want to punish someone.'

'Me,' Reilly said morosely.

'The question is,' Lucie said. 'Who stole them?'

Bodie stared around the place. 'Whoever it was left us with a big fat nothing. Damn, this is bad news.'

'Let's check around,' Cassidy said.

They split up and started checking the place. Bodie went to the far wall, where the paintings had been, and started rooting through the discarded sheets. Reilly joined him. They discovered nothing underneath, nothing except rotting material. Bodie found himself enveloped in a dust cloud.

Around the warehouse, the others searched. They worked tentatively, unsure what they would find, but proficiently. Cassidy came across a bronze statue that Reilly didn't recognise. Jemma and Lucie found some old fairground paraphernalia. Yasmine found nothing but another pile of old sheets. Heidi checked through one of the far windows, making sure they were still alone.

Bodie stared at the emptiness. This was quite unusual. Reilly then clicked his fingers.

'The motion cameras,' he said. 'We can see what they picked up.'

Bodie nodded. He had been thinking along the same lines. He followed Reilly to one of the far walls. Sitting right there, on a dust-strewn shelf, was a mains fed camera disguised as a plastic figure. The figure was tatty and wouldn't attract attention. As Bodie leaned closer, he saw the lens buried inside the figure.

'Two,' Reilly indicated another figure a bit further along. 'I came prepared so that I can plug them into my phone.'

Working quickly, Reilly produced a cable. He picked up one of the plastic figures and inserted one end of the cable into its back. Then he connected the other end to his phone. The screen switched instantly to the view of the warehouse.

'Good, it's still working,' Reilly said. 'Now let's delve deeper. The cameras work on motion sensors.'

Using the controls, he scrolled backwards and forwards through footage, looking for any sign of the intruders. Of course, there wasn't a lot of footage to be seen – the warehouse being empty. The sequence he was looking for came up relatively quickly.

'There,' he said.

Bodie watched as dark, hulking figures entered the camera's eyeline, as they made their way across to the bulky sheets where Reilly and his companions had clearly hidden the paintings.

'Who the hell are they?' Reilly squinted.

Faces turned towards the camera as the newcomers explored the entire warehouse. Bodie counted five in total, some of them coming right up to the camera. In the background, a man who was clearly the boss gesticulated and started shouting something. Soon, all five men were rooting among Reilly's treasure.

'Bastards,' Reilly said with feeling.

Bodie didn't remind him he'd stolen it in the first place. He watched the figures.

'Do you recognise any of them?' he asked.

Reilly, peering hard at the screen, shook his head. 'Not so far. That big guy – the leader – looks vaguely familiar, but I can't place him.'

With little hope, the others all took a closer look, but they didn't know the robbers either. He watched as Reilly downloaded the footage to his phone.

'It's all we have,' he said after a while. 'They break in, look around and spend half an hour stealing the paintings. That's me done. I'm dead.'

'Maybe you could forward the footage on to the Diablos,' Cassidy suggested. 'They might recognise the people. And there's proof that the paintings were stolen.'

Reilly took a deep breath. 'Same problem as before. They won't let it go at that. They'll want more from me.'

'So what the hell are we going to do?' Jemma asked.

'We work with what we've got,' Bodie said, and then pointed at Reilly's phone. 'The footage.'

Lucie looked confused. 'But we don't know who they are.'

'We don't,' Bodie said. 'Doesn't mean someone else won't.'

'That sounds like you have an idea,' Reilly turned to him expectantly.

Bodie nodded. 'What we need is someone with access to facial rec. Those men in that footage – they're criminals clearly. There's a good chance their faces are in some database somewhere. If we can somehow get access to that database...'

'That's a great idea,' Reilly said. 'But who...?'

'My old mate,' Bodie said. 'Jack Pantera.'

CHAPTER EIGHT

They departed the warehouse with care and made their way back to the hotel. Once there, they reassembled in the hotel's twenty-four-hour bar area and sat in the semi-dark with drinks to hand. It was Bodie who took the phone out of his pocket and made the call.

'Jack?' he asked when the call was answered. 'Is that you?'

Jack Pantera was Bodie's old mentor, the man who had taken him from being a young tearaway and turned him into a responsible, careful, highly capable thief. The man was currently living under CIA protection somewhere near Miami and he and Bodie hadn't spoken in years.

'Guy? Is that you?'

'Yeah, Jack, it's me. Long time no speak. How's tricks?'

'Ah, you know me. Nothing's changed much.'

'You still in the same situation?'

'With our friends? Yeah, I don't think that'll ever change. You did well to escape from under that shadow.'

Bodie was well aware of it. 'You still up to your old tricks?'

'Haha, in the full view of our friends? You must

be joking. Now, why did you call me, Guy? I know it's not just to shoot the shit.'

Bodie thought briefly that it was a shame he hadn't called Pantera just to 'shoot the shit.' They were old friends, and old friends deserved to stay in touch. They could be a balm for the soul.

'I may need some of your contacts,' he said.

'Just say the word.'

'Can I speak freely?'

'As far as I know, the phones aren't tapped. But who really knows these days? It's a chance you take.'

'Oh, that's reassuring.'

He could almost see Jack Pantera shrug. 'I've had some near the knuckle conversations on here. No repercussions yet.'

Bodie decided to jump right in. 'We're trying to track someone down. We have video footage. How're your facial recognition contacts these days?'

'Are they criminals?'

'We think so, yeah. They robbed some paintings from...' he stopped suddenly, deciding he didn't want to risk too much information. 'Well, they stole paintings,' he ended weakly.

He waited for Pantera to reply, sinking down further into his plush seat. They were all seated on their own comfy chairs, drinks to hand; the lights turned low all around them so that the only real glows of light came from behind the bar. The windows were bare and they could see speckles of light outside from the street, unfocused.

'Do you have the footage with you?'

'Yeah, sure. It's on a phone.'

'I can work with that. Is there anything specific you're looking for?'

'Just names. Maybe affiliations. There're five guys on the tape. Maybe they're mercs, maybe they work together all the time. Maybe they work for someone else. That's the kind of thing we're looking for.'

'I can do that. Email the footage to me.'

Bodie waved at Reilly and gave him an email address. 'Send it,' he said.

Pantera waited patiently at the other end until he received the message. 'Got it,' he said. 'Now let's hope my contacts remember me.'

'As if they could forget,' Bodie laughed.

'Hey, I'm not that bad. At least, not anymore.'

Pantera sounded wistful, and slightly upset, as if he felt like a dog working with dentures in place of real teeth. Bodie sipped his drink, waiting for something more forceful from Pantera, but it didn't come. Maybe the man really was as chilled out as he sounded. If so, it was a surprise to Bodie. Pantera had once been one of London's most influential criminals.

'How long will it take you, Jack?' he asked.

'Hopefully, a few hours. It's early evening here. If my guy's still at work, I'll be back soon.'

Bodie ended the call and looked at Reilly. 'He's the best chance we've got. I'm pretty sure he'll ID those guys. The question is – what do we do then?'

Reilly looked thoughtful. 'I think we need to know who we're dealing with first. The problem is – none of this helps me.'

'Not yet,' Bodie said. 'But we are making some progress.'

'Not as much as I'd hoped,' Reilly said. 'If the paintings had still been there...' he left it hanging.

The team sat in reflective silence, none of them in a good mood. This was a situation that, on first look, had appeared comparatively easy to resolve. A quick trip to Prague, doing what they do best by entering the warehouse, reveal the paintings to the authorities. Easy.

But that had all changed.

Bodie had enough faith in Pantera to stay in the bar that night. He could have gone upstairs, gone to bed, tried to get some much needed sleep. But he was too wired now, too expectant. He – and the others – felt as if something was about to happen. Bodie knew Pantera would come through.

Two hours later, he did.

CHAPTER NINE

Bodie's phone rang, shattering the silent stillness that hung heavy in the twenty-four-hour bar.

'Jack?' he answered, recognising the number.

'The very same. It must be late there.'

'About three a.m. Been waiting for your call.'

'Are you all there? How's Cassidy and Jemma?'

Bodie was tempted to pass the phone around, let them catch up for a while, but one look at Reilly's expectant face changed his mind.

'They're good as ever, mate. Do you have anything for me?'

'Straight to it, I see. You don't change. I mailed the footage to a friend of mine who, luckily, was still at work. He came back pretty quickly.'

'Did he ID the men?'

'Yeah, mate, yes, he did. You've got five very dangerous individuals there.'

Reilly was listening to the conversation, and now his face fell. Bodie listened harder. 'Who are they?'

'Right. Well, there's a guy called Collins. Another named West. But you don't need the full list. All you need to know is this. They all work for the damn Petrov gang.'

'The Petrovs?' Bodie repeated. 'I've never heard of them.'

'They work for a *gang?*' Reilly said, aghast. 'Shit.'

'I'm surprised you've never heard of the Petrovs,' Pantera said. 'They're notorious. Very nasty. I could tell you a few horror stories.'

'I've heard of them,' Reilly said. 'They're a rival to the Diablos.'

Bodie turned to him. 'You're kidding? They're a *rival?* So...you think they did this to spite the Diablos?'

'It's possible.'

'The Petrovs are pure killers,' Pantera went on. 'They once found out someone had betrayed them, was in fact betraying them at that very minute, in a police station in Sofia. They turned all their might on that station immediately, sent all their men to wipe it out and make an example of the traitor. Later, they found him strung up to the sign outside, his hands and feet on the ground below. Another time, they took exception to an article written in the local paper about them. They attacked the paper's offices, burned it to the ground, and nailed its boss and three editors to the walls. A few of them got convicted, but there are always more. The Petrovs, I'm afraid...they believe they're above the law.'

'Where do they hang out?'

'Bulgaria. Near Sofia. They work the capital.'

'How extensive are they?'

'I'd guess in the hundreds. They're well connected, well funded, just like the Diablos.'

'And speaking of the Diablos,' Bodie turned to Reilly. 'You say they're rivals. How could that be?'

'It happened whilst I was running with the gang,' Reilly said. 'The Diablos were dealing drugs in Prague, had a sizeable chunk of the city under their control. Nothing happened there without their say so and they were pretty untouchable. Anyway, the Petrovs muscled their way in, started a gang war that spilled over into the streets. Dozen of Diablos died, and there's been bad blood ever since. The Diablos and the Petrovs run Prague's drug trade alongside each other now. It's a hate-hate relationship.'

'So the Petrovs stole the paintings from the Diablos' warehouse,' Bodie ran through the facts. 'The Petrovs haven't told the Diablos. Presumably, they haven't sold the paintings either. What do they want with them?'

'Could be anything from one-upmanship to some grand plan,' Pantera said. 'The problem is the Petrovs have a lot of property. They have places all over the city. It's not like there's a house you can go to and the stash will be there. All I can say is, be very careful. They wouldn't hesitate to kill first and ask questions later.'

Bodie felt as if they were floundering. They didn't know the Petrovs, did not know where they hung out, where their headquarters were. Obviously they didn't have a clue where the paintings might be stashed, or even why the Petrovs had stolen them.

'Fells like we're back to square one,' he said.

'It's worse than that,' Reilly said. 'We know who we're up against, and we stand no chance.'

'Oh, I wouldn't say that,' Pantera said with a smile in his voice.

Reilly blinked. 'Why not?'

'Don't you know who you're dealing with here?'

Bodie shifted and then grinned. 'We're the relic hunters,' he said. 'We've been in some damn tight situations before. It's not easy, but there's always a way.'

Reilly looked grateful. 'Thanks for sticking with me in this. You know you don't have to. You're putting yourselves in great danger.'

'Hey, we're a team,' Cassidy said. 'And you're part of it. We'll stand by you.'

Reilly bowed his head. Bodie turned his attention back to Pantera. 'Can you give us any more information about these Petrovs?'

'The head guy is called Cezar Petrov. He has three brothers who rule ruthlessly at his side. Together, they control everything. Drugs. Prostitution. Arms. You name it, they're firmly ensconced.'

'Do you have any contacts with the Bulgarian police? Someone who could give us a few pointers?'

But, Bodie saw, this operation would not be easy at all. 'No,' Pantera told them. 'I don't.'

'Bollocks.'

'Apart from one thing.'

Bodie smiled to himself. It was typical Pantera, saving the best nugget for last. He didn't say a word, waiting the guy out.

Jemma crumbled. 'Which is?'

'My contact knew of one of their places in Sofia. It's an old train yard from which they run several of their operations. You can use it as a starting point. I know I don't have to tell you to be careful.'

Bodie asked him for the address and then wrote it down. Pantera wound the conversation up and promised to call more often. Bodie did the same. It was a shame to let their old friendship deteriorate and, whilst neither of them did it on purpose, that was sometimes the way of the world. New endeavours, the weight of work, pressure…it all got in the way. He and Pantera would always be the best of friends, but that didn't mean they'd contact each other often.

When the call ended, Bodie looked around the table. He checked his watch. 'It's after three,' he said. 'How about we kip for the rest of the night, grab a late breakfast, and then head to Sofia? We can easily find the train yard after we land.'

'And then what?' Reilly said.

Cassidy was quick to answer. 'We do what we always do,' she said. 'Make it up as we go along.'

They smiled, finished their drinks, and headed up to their rooms. They were all dog tired. Bodie was asleep almost as soon as his head hit the pillow. He didn't dwell on what was to come, didn't worry too much about the Petrovs.

They had beat overwhelming odds before. They would do so again.

He hoped.

CHAPTER TEN

Sofia was bustling and sprawling, a trendy yet historical city awash with locals and tourists alike. Bodie and the team landed safely and immediately rented two cars and made their way through the city centre's mass to the train yard in question. It was a tedious journey, but the team stayed mostly quiet, thinking about what they had to do.

The train yard was a chaotic space, full of rusting old hulks, twisted tracks that were either piled in a corner or clawing, warped, at the air to one side of the vast compound. To Bodie's mind they looked like desperate, broken fingers, trying to grab the attention of anyone who would set them free. A high, chain-link fence surrounded the place, also rusted and topped with barbed wire. The gates were barely hanging on, attached to the fence by threads. Bodie saw several old carriages dotted around and an engine surrounded by parts, as if the mechanic had had every intention of rebuilding and then just given up.

The main building stretched for about three hundred yards, a two-storey structure with fresh glass and a new roof. Clearly, someone had been up keeping the building. The door was wide and sturdy and there was another roller shutter mechanism further along. Bodie parked his car along the busy street outside and watched as Yasmine pulled in behind. It was a bright blue day, their vision not marred by anything. Bodie watched the train yard.

They spent some time in position. The train yard was on the other side of the street. Pedestrians passed by constantly, a flow of disordered humanity, helping conceal Bodie's and the others' intentions. Cars were also a constant up and down the main road.

Bodie watched the train yards doors and windows. He saw movement through the glass, saw several figures coming and going. The roller shutter doors were in use, and several men clad in dark jackets wandered through them and then went back inside. Some stopped for a smoke, others to walk around the yard as if taking a break. Some huddled together and laughed and joked before heading back inside.

'It's well populated,' Cassidy said after a while. 'Petrov's men are everywhere.'

The building was indeed busy, the action never stopping. About an hour after they started watching the front gates were opened to admit a large white van. This van disgorged four men, who quickly disappeared inside the building and then left. The gate was left open and soon other vehicles appeared, coming and going.

'There's no security,' Cassidy observed. 'Looks like anyone can get in or out at the drop of a hat.'

Bodie had noticed that. 'We can certainly get inside,' he said. 'It's what we do when we get there that counts.'

Reilly was in the same car. 'Of course, because

this isn't their only property. The paintings could be anywhere.'

'So what's the play?' Heidi said from the front seat.

Bodie had been watching the roller shutter and its occasional lurker. 'They exit that way,' he pointed. 'When they want a smoke or a chat break. Occasionally, loners perhaps, go for a stroll around the yard.'

Heidi looked over at him. 'You're thinking we snag one?'

Bodie shrugged. 'Can't hurt.'

'It could,' she said. 'What if we snag one who doesn't know the location of the paintings? If we do that, we're all out of luck.'

'Can you think of a better idea?'

Heidi looked back at the train yard, saw how busy it was, the amount of people traffic coming and going. Even if they did brashly enter through the front gates, they'd still have to ask someone where the paintings were being kept.

'I guess it poses the least risk to us,' she said after a while.

'We can't all go,' Reilly pointed out. 'A couple, maybe. And me.'

'Why you?'

'Because I'm the most invested in this. I can even verify what he's telling us by asking him for details about the paintings. Also, I want to feel like I'm being useful.'

Bodie watched for a while longer. Two hours passed. During that time he saw just two men go for a stroll around the train yard. 'The question is,' he said. 'Do we go by day or by night?'

'We can't guarantee they'll do it at night,' Cassidy said. 'I say we go now.'

Bodie agreed. Together, they climbed out of the car; the others following. Bodie looked surprised. 'It's just me, Cass and Reilly.'

'How are we supposed to know that?' Heidi asked. 'And why?'

Bodie shrugged. 'Always been that way,' he said. 'Don't worry. Jemma would be next on the pecking order, then you. It's due to length of service.'

Heidi gave him a look as if she couldn't decide if he was messing with her, but didn't query his decision any more. Soon, Bodie had approached the other car and told them the plan. All they had to do was sit tight.

Minutes later, Bodie was ready. He, Cassidy and Reilly started walking up the pavement in parallel to the train yard, inspecting its fence. A hundred yards further up the road, they crossed so that they were now on the same side.

Bodie waited until they were situated behind a pile of old rusted machine parts, out of view of the building's windows. He then lingered until the pavement was clear of pedestrians and just the odd car passing by. Quickly then, he grabbed hold of the fence and started climbing. He laid his jacket over the top, protecting himself from the barbed wire, and jumped down the other side. The entire process took seconds.

He crouched, staying hidden behind the machine parts. Cassidy came next, scurrying up the fence like a squirrel and leaping over, landing gracefully at his side. Together, the two of them met Reilly's intense gaze through the metal links.

'Your turn,' Bodie said.

Reilly waited for a break in people and cars, the moments stretching to minutes. At first, he couldn't catch a break. There was always someone or something coming. Then, as Bodie started to get anxious, the moment arrived, and he hit the fence hard, climbing swiftly. He hopped over the top and was then crouching beside them among the machinery.

Together, they turned towards the building.

'Let's get into position,' Bodie said.

They already knew the general route the men took when they went for a stroll. Bodie now led the way to that area, staying low and away from the view of the windows. They flitted from machine parts to a carriage and made their way around it. Next up were some crates, behind which Bodie crouched and waited. He turned to the others.

'We'll wait it out here.'

His words were an omen, and they certainly did have a wait. An hour passed. Bodie kept an eye on the building between holes in the piles of crates, watching expectantly. Men came and went through the shutter doors, but none came for a stroll.

He checked his watch. It was late afternoon. The sunshine was as bright as ever, picking every little detail out. He tried not to move around too much so that no one would notice his movements behind the crates. Cassidy and Reilly, beside him, were equally impatient.

'Damn, this is taking forever,' Reilly said.

Bodie shrugged. 'Like I said before, can you think of a better idea?'

'We can't exactly walk right in there and start asking questions,' Cassidy said.

'Yeah, yeah, I get it.'

Another hour passed, and they were becoming even more restless. Bodie had had to find a place where they could stretch their legs. It wasn't much of a space, but it did the trick. He was just coming back from easing the pressure on his joints when Reilly held up a hand.

'Wait,' he said. 'Someone's coming.'

Bodie crouched at his side, peering through the gaps. Sure enough, a tall guy wearing glasses and a beard had exited through the shutter door and was heading their way. He kicked at the ground as he came, sauntering, whistling a soulless tune. His eyes were on the ground and he didn't look happy.

Bodie made ready, knowing this was their one chance. Cassidy and Reilly rose next to him. They watched the approaching man carefully.

When the man came around the pile of crates, Bodie leapt at him. He grabbed his throat and squeezed to stop any sound, then punched him in the solar plexus. The man's face turned from surprise to pain, and then he collapsed to his knees. Bodie went with him, still clutching his throat.

'Not a sound,' he whispered, glaring into the man's eyes.

There was a frightened nod. Bodie could tell instantly that this man was no fighter. He pulled him into deeper concealment.

'Now,' he said. 'We have a few questions for you.'

He loosened his grip on the throat.

'Please, please,' the man said. 'I just work in the office. I have no gun, no knife. My only weapon is a pencil sharpener.'

It was intended to lighten the situation, and

showed that the man wasn't as scared as he looked. Bodie punched him in the middle again, showing that he meant business.

'You don't answer, you die,' he said simply. 'Is that simple enough for you?'

The man stared at them through terrified eyes. 'What do you want to know?'

It occurred to Bodie then that he hadn't really thought of the right way to phrase his questions. He trawled quickly through the possibilities.

'All right,' he said finally. 'You work for the Petrov gang, right?'

The man nodded, eyes wide.

Bodie loosened his grip some more. 'The Petrovs stole some works of art, some paintings, including four Rembrandts from a warehouse belonging to the Diablos. We want to know where those paintings are being stored.'

A look of recognition passed across the man's face, but was quickly hidden. Cassidy saw it and held up half a brick.

'This bad boy is gonna get up close and personal with your nose if you don't come clean,' she said.

The man tried to speak, but then made a noise, presumably because Bodie's hand was too tight. Bodie loosed it some more, barely touching him now. As he did so, the man exploded into action, shooting a jab up at Bodie's chin that caught him by surprise. He fell back, shocked.

Damn, he had underestimated the bastard.

The bearded man struck again, two fast short stiffened-finger jabs that hit Bodie's midriff and throat, and made him collapse to the ground, choking. The guy was good. He rose swiftly to his feet, turned to yell out something that would attract his colleagues.

Cassidy smashed him on the back of the head with the brick. He staggered but didn't go down. Cassidy followed her attack up with a hard knee to the spine and then hooked her arm around the man's throat. The guy struggled, but she had him in a grip of steel.

She hauled him backwards, dragging him off his feet, holding him by his throat. 'Don't fucking move,' she whispered.

The man slumped in her grip. She relented slightly, her mouth close to his right ear. 'Now,' she said. 'Answer the question.'

'I don't know-'

Reilly came around to the front of the man and started hammering punches at his ribs as if he was a punching bag. The man kicked weakly and jerked in Cassidy's iron hold.

Bodie, by now, had struggled back to his feet. He let out a few breaths and held his throat, feeling the residual pain. He coughed. 'That hurt,' he said. 'So you are a fighter. Okay then. We'll treat you like one.'

Reilly kept punching. Cassidy kept squeezing. Together, they took the fight right out of the man. He kicked weakly and made pitiful noises. Cassidy dragged him to the pile of crates and sat him up with his back to them, her knuckles clenched before his eyes.

'No more messing about,' she said. 'You answer or it's gonna get much worse.'

'The...the...winery,' he said weakly, holding several broken ribs. 'It's...it's...on the outskirts of

Sofia, an estate,' he gave them an address. 'The paintings have been there since we stole them. I've seen them in the cellar.'

Bodie stared at him. The guy was in agony, face twisted, gasping. It sounded like the truth and probably was. At least, it sounded plausible.

'I don't believe you,' he said. 'Reilly, work on those ribs some more.'

Reilly bent down, ready to deliver more blows. The bearded man held out a hand and emitted several gasps. 'No, no, it is true,' his accent was getting thicker as his fear deepened. 'I have seen them. They are there.'

'Describe them to me,' Reilly said threateningly.

'Well, they're paintings. Some are of the sea, others are buildings. There's a bunch of flowers on one. The frames are all dark and thick, ribbed maybe. The biggest painting shows a castle with a full moon behind it.'

Reilly stepped back. 'He's telling the truth. At least, insofar as he's seen the paintings.'

Bodie stepped on the man's ankle, hard. 'If you're lying about the location, we'll be back for you. We'll make a point of finding you.'

'They are there, in the cellar, at the winery. I am not lying to you.'

Bodie believed him. He nodded and looked at Cassidy. 'Do your stuff.'

'I wouldn't tell anyone about this,' she whispered in the man's ear. 'They'll probably kill you for incompetence.'

And then she smashed him in the left temple, rendering him unconscious. She let him slip to the ground and looked behind them.

'Shall we get the hell out of here?'

'I think now would be a good time,' Bodie said.

'Just remember the address,' Reilly said. 'I don't want to have to come back here and do this all again.'

With a grim smile, Bodie led the way back to the fence. The three of them stayed low and ran fast, using the obstacles once again to hide them. Soon, they were at the fence and debating what to do. It was busy.

'Fuck it,' Bodie said. 'We all climb at once and leg it for the car. We've got what we need.'

Together, they leapt for the fence.

CHAPTER ELEVEN

The winery was a vast estate surrounded by low hedges and stands of trees. There was no fence because of the size and there was a wide, gravelled, winding driveway that led from the road to the main house. Bodie and the others drove past it slowly, getting a feel for the place. There were several other buildings dotted about the land, but they already knew they didn't need to worry about those.

It was the cellars of the main building they were after.

'We gonna steal these paintings back?' Cassidy asked from the back seat of the car.

'That's what we're good at,' Bodie said.

'*Used* to be good at,' Cassidy said. 'The jury's out on the present day.'

Bodie shrugged. 'Touche, I guess.'

'Well, I've never stolen anything in my life,' Heidi said. 'I don't know how I feel about doing this.'

'But you used to work for the CIA,' Cassidy said with mock astonishment. 'Isn't that exactly what they do?'

'Funny. Since I met the relic hunters, I've done more criminal activities than at any other time in my life.'

'Most of that whilst still under the CIA's directorship,' Bodie reminded her.

Heidi shrugged. Bodie made the drive past the whole estate and then turned around to come back the other way. The long winding drive was tree-lined and so were the grounds that led up to the house. There was no sign of any security patrols or cameras. Bodie made two more passes and then drove them to the nearest parking area where they could leave the cars and converse.

'It's getting close to dark,' Yasmine said first. 'We can't do much more recon today.'

'Agreed,' Bodie said. 'We've driven past the house enough already. I don't want to risk doing it again today. So...what have we come up with?'

The team started brainstorming ideas based on what they'd seen. The main house was entirely approachable, but they had no way of knowing what was inside, nor how many men. During their drives they had seen no signs of activity.

'So we're going to have to do this all again tomorrow,' Jemma said.

'We need as much information as we can get,' Bodie reminded her. 'And...if we can't see them, they can't see us.'

Jemma smiled. 'Not entirely true.'

'I saw no cameras, no surveillance,' Lucie said.

'We're missing the big picture,' Heidi said in a worried voice. 'You want to steal the paintings, yeah? Well, we can't carry the damn things out of there one at a time, can we?'

Bodie nodded. 'I was saving that discussion until we knew a little more.'

The others stared gloomily from face to face. 'It is a bit of an impasse,' Jemma said.

They climbed back into their cars, drove to a

hotel, and spent the night. The next day, fed and rested and watered, they were back driving past the winery. On their third pass Bodie found himself stuck behind a small truck, one that slowed and turned into the winding driveway. On the side it read: Union Winery. It trundled into the estate, slowing as it reached the main building and drove past to one of the other, smaller structures. Bodie now noticed several other trucks parked there in haphazard fashion. From this distance, it looked like they were being loaded with crates.

'They bottle the wine here, box it, and ship it out,' he said. 'It's still a working plant.'

'How does that help us?' Cassidy asked.

'Maybe not at all.'

The morning passed as they made long looping passes of the estate. In summary, they saw three trucks of varying sizes and two cars head up the driveway. Still, nobody patrolled the grounds, but they did see a woman in front of the house, talking on her phone. They also saw several figures by the trucks, bringing out boxes and crates of, presumably, wine. The house looked old and shabby, its gutters hanging in one place. There were several cars parked to the side in the same position as yesterday, which suggested quite a few people lived there. Finally, on the last run, Yasmine got a glimpse of a guard walking around the side of the house. The man carried a gun.

When they met up at the parking area again, they shared notes.

'So, it's highly dangerous,' Heidi said. 'And we have no way of knowing what to expect. No way of transporting the treasure. No clean getaway. Couldn't be better.'

'Sounds perfect,' Bodie grinned.

'We've faced worse odds,' Cassidy said. 'But we do need a plan.'

'Well, it's easy enough to access the estate,' Reilly said. 'We can drive close by, use one of the little lay-bys to park the cars, and sneak in. I know you guys could access the house. After that, we don't know where the cellars are or a good way to steal back the treasure.'

'It'll be all about confidence,' Bodie said. 'Balls.'

'Balls?' Cassidy looked confused.

Bodie gave her a weary look. She knew exactly what he meant. 'We're just gonna have to blag it,' he said.

'You have a plan?' Jemma asked.

Bodie nodded. 'I do,' he said. 'You see the trucks?'

Jemma nodded.

'They're loading at the back of the property, right? Where the wine's being produced. But I've seen two truck's load at the side of the house too. They must be taking wine out of the cellars and selling it. The good stuff.'

Cassidy stared at him. 'I'm getting a bad feeling here.'

'You know it,' Bodie couldn't help but smile. 'There's an acceptable reason for a truck being close to the house where the cellars are. All we need is a truck.'

'If I remember rightly, there were drivers in all of those trucks,' Lucie said.

Bodie leaned on the roof of their car. He nodded. 'That's unlucky for them,' he said.

'They could be armed,' Cassidy pointed out.

Bodie shrugged. 'Can you think of a better idea? I mean…it's the closest we can get to the house, and there's a reason for us being there.'

'How big are those paintings?' Lucie suddenly asked, thinking hard.

Reilly held his hands apart. 'Not big,' he said. 'Standard size, I think.'

'What I'm asking, I guess, is can we carry one each?'

'Yeah, easily.'

'And there's thirteen of them. Seven of us. Two trips each. That's…not much more than ten or fifteen minutes if we make it quick. Maybe it is achievable.'

'Like I said,' Bodie continued. 'If anyone has a better idea, speak up now.'

The team stood around, looking at each other. Cassidy didn't look happy and didn't hide her misgivings. Jemma and Lucie gave him hesitant looks. Heidi was staring back at the house, and Reilly and Yasmine talked quietly to each other. Bodie waited.

'Are we agreed?' He asked finally. 'Because there's no time like the present.'

Cassidy shaded her eyes as she looked back in the direction of the house. 'It's damn risky,' she said.

Bodie nodded. It *was* risky, but it was all they could do. If they chose the right truck, they'd only have to deal with the driver and they had enough brawn between them to make that work. He didn't want to hurt the guy too much, just keep him quiet. Once they had the paintings, they could drive them into the city, hide out, and alert the cops to their existence. It wasn't exactly a smooth as silk operation, but it didn't have to be. All they had to do was give the paintings back to the authorities. And if that meant robbing a local gang...

Bodie was up for it. He looked around. They all were. There wasn't any point in wasting any more time.

'Good,' he said. 'Time to go.'

CHAPTER TWELVE

First, they needed a few supplies. They drove partway back towards the city, found a hardware store and made a few purchases. Then, they drove back into place before heading out again, finding a quiet lay-by and leaving the cars. They found some cover in the form of trees and hedgerows and made their way closer to the house, staying out of sight. When a vehicle passed along the road, they melted into the undergrowth. Bodie soon found himself crouching among trees, staring into the grounds of the house and watching the trucks load their cargos.

The team studied the process for a while. It looked like a well-oiled machine. The drivers pulled up, showed their papers to a supervisor, then got back into the cab as men used forklifts to load crates of wine into the backs of their trucks. When the loading was complete, the supervisor came around to the front and waved at the driver.

'We can't hit them during the loading,' Cassidy whispered at his side. 'There's too many people around.'

'Agreed. But they do take their time trundling up the long driveway. And I'm guessing there's a solid hour or so between trucks. That's all the time we need.'

Bodie explained the plan and then started leading them around to the front of the house. The going was tough in places, the undergrowth thick and tangled, almost impassable. The sun beat down from above and there was the scent of wildflowers in the air.

Bodie ignored it all, intent on one thing. At his side, Reilly pushed them just as hard.

As they reached the front of the property, they slowed, checking again for security and, especially, cameras. They saw none. The gates were open, admitting the trucks on a regular basis, and there were no guards. Bodie crouched behind the brick gateposts for a while, looking down the driveway.

'Clear,' he said. 'Come on.'

They ran into the property, their boots crunching on gravel, and then once more found the undergrowth at the side of the road. Bodie hid behind a hedge, the others alongside him. 'Now,' he said. 'We wait.'

It took almost thirty minutes, but soon they heard the sound of a truck lumbering in their direction. Bodie popped his head up, saw an old dust-strewn Mercedes rattling up the road. Through the front window, he saw a driver at the wheel, no passenger. He nodded and turned to the others.

'This is it.'

They braced for action. Bodie went first, stepping out into the open and holding up a hand. He walked and stood as if he was meant to be there, just another guard or worker protecting the property.

The truck slowed, the driver's head bobbing. He flung up a hand in protest. Bodie went around to the side of the truck and reached up to rap on the window.

'Open up!' He yelled.

The door was flung open, almost catching Bodie on the side of the head. The guy yelled something unintelligible that Bodie didn't understand, then brandished some papers at him, looking extremely irate.

Bodie gestured for the man to get out of the truck and then spoke in English again just to help confuse matters. The driver let out a long sigh and then climbed down to the ground. The truck itself was still idling, the sides gently vibrating.

'Thank you,' Bodie said, and then produced a large penknife. He held the blade to the man's throat. The guy's eyes went wide, and he started blinking, his mouth working but no words coming out.

There was a rush of feet, and then the entire team was at Bodie's side. Cassidy had a length of rope, which she used to tie the driver's hands together. Then, they bundled him into the passenger seat footwell and warned him to stay quiet with gestures rather than words. As Cassidy did that, the others were opening up the rear doors.

Bodie raced around to the back. Inside, he saw several stacks of boxes, all stamped with the same label. There was still room inside for thirteen paintings though, he guessed. Plenty of room. He watched as the others climbed up into the truck, and then raced back around to the front, jumped up into the driver's seat.

Bodie swiftly turned the truck around and started heading back towards the house. He knew where to go because of their earlier surveillance and didn't waste any time heading there now. He passed the front of the house, seeing no one around, then turned left at the far end. A short road ran beside the house, which he drove down now and then turned around again so that he was facing the right way to get out.

Now, he was parked at the side of the house. A closed door stood to his right. Bodie warned the passenger once more and then jumped down from the truck. He paused for a moment to check around.

Over to the left, partially hidden by trees, stood the wine warehouse where, even now, a truck was being loaded. Bodie could hear the activity. To the right, the main house stood. In front, there was nothing but greenery and lawns that led to the front of the property. Behind, saw a low slung building that could have been a garage.

There was nobody around.

Thankful, Bodie closed the truck door and started rushing towards the back so that he could safely open the doors. As he did so, he came face to face with a short, wide man with a bristling beard.

Bodie cursed inwardly. Damn all the luck.

The man challenged him, muttering something Bodie didn't understand. He nodded, smiled, and replied in English. The guy frowned but didn't seem to mind. He slapped the side of the truck and then gestured to the cab.

Bodie cringed inside. The last thing he wanted to do was show this man the inside of the cab. It'd be hard to explain the trussed up driver.

The man started walking towards the door.

Bodie swallowed hard and then stayed behind him. He readied a blow that would hopefully knock the guy unconscious, brought an arm up.

The man whirled and held out a hand. Bodie blinked at him. For a moment there was an uneasy standoff, and then something hit Bodie.

He was asking for the papers!

Bodie nodded. The only problem was the papers were on the driver's seat. He cracked open the door, didn't open it far, conscious of how close the short man was to discovering the driver. He reached in, grabbed the sheaf of papers and pulled them out before pushing the door closed again. The guy showed no interest in looking inside the cab.

He studied the papers, frowning. Then he waved them in Bodie's face. Were they the wrong papers?

'That's all they gave me,' he said with a blank look. 'Are they not for the house?' He tried to look confused.

The man studied them again. He, too, looked confused now. He spoke again in his language, something that Bodie couldn't make out.

'It's a mystery,' he said. 'Maybe you should just let us get on with our job.' He gestured at the truck and the house, trying to convey that very fact.

The short guy finally let out a long sigh and then thrust the papers back at Bodie. He waved and started stalking off, shaking his head. Bodie hoped to hell he wasn't going off to look for some supervisor, and then decided it was now or never.

Risking it, he ran to the back of the truck and flung the doors wide open. The others peered out at him, blinking in the light, also looking confused.

'What the hell's going on?' Cassidy asked.

'Company,' Bodie said. 'He's gone now.'

'For good?'

'Well, I didn't hurt him. We're gonna have to make this quick.'

They jumped out of the truck and made their way to the side door of the house. Bodie had a dreadful moment where he imagined the doors being locked, but when Jemma pushed on them, they opened inwards. The team crowded inside.

To face a small polished kitchen with lots of silver surfaces and a far door. To the right stood another door, this one shabby and pockmarked. Jemma ran to it and pushed. Beyond sat a set of stairs.

'Cellar door,' she said. 'Has to be.'

They started down after Bodie found a light switch. The steps were concrete and wide, bowed in the middle because of endless wear and tear. They followed the steps down for a while; the air becoming colder and colder.

At the bottom, Bodie stepped off into a wide, well-illuminated space. There were endless wine racks reaching up to the ceiling, standing haphazardly everywhere. No orderly rows here. It looked like the person who designed it had had one too many bottles of the stuff that lined the shelves. From his vantage point, he couldn't see any of the four walls.

'I guess we split up,' he said. 'Shout when you find something.'

The team hurried off, splitting up through the various racks of shelving. Bodie went to the right, following a path through the racks, keeping a close eye out for a bunch of paintings. Minutes passed. He went by endless, dusty racks, all starkly illuminated. He kept an ear out for the others, and for anyone else who might inadvertently join them. Maybe they should position a crate of wine at the foot of the stairs as cover just in case someone found them.

Ahead, he now saw the far wall. Nestled against it were several shrouded shapes. Bodie ran to them, throwing back the sheets. Dust filled the air and his lungs, and all he found were several battered, empty crates. He cursed silently.

Long minutes passed, each one adding to the tension that filled him. What if someone else came along and found the truck? What if the same guy came back? What if they found the driver? The questions and the anxiety ate at him.

He set off back a different way, using the far wall as a guide. Still nothing from the others. He realised he could see the far stairs from his current vantage point, and their emptiness was reassuring.

But there were seven of them down here searching and, just then, there was a shout. Lucie.

Bodie ran towards the sound, heart beating fast. Lucie sounded excited. She shouted a couple more times to guide them in, and then Bodie could see her at the end of a passageway, looking around.

He raced to her side. Soon, the others had joined them. Lucie gestured at the wall and the pile of paintings just resting there.

'Not even covered,' she said. 'They're just dumped here.' She turned to Reilly. 'Are these your paintings?'

Reilly's eyes were wide. 'Yeah,' he said, counting. 'All thirteen of them.'

Bodie bent down and grabbed one. 'Let's get this done.'

CHAPTER THIRTEEN

The team rushed the paintings back up the stairs, taking care not to damage them along the way. Bodie sprinted up the steps and raced out into the kitchen. The doors were open as they'd left them, and the truck was still there. He exited the house and ran to the back of the truck. The team streamed after him. Reilly was the first to jump up into the truck and start reaching down for items. Too slowly, the first seven paintings were handed up and stowed in the back.

Bodie stepped back, about to go running back into the house. As he did so, there was a crunch of gravel and two figures came into sight.

They walked around the side of the truck – the same short, wide man and this time he'd brought a friend. The other man was his opposite, tall and skinny and sporting a full head of hair. Both men carried guns on their belts but their hands weren't near them, signalling they weren't overly suspicious – at least for the moment.

Bodie managed a wide smile. 'Hello again,' he said.

The short man gestured to the tall man and said something intelligible. Next, the tall man spoke.

'I speak English,' he said, causing Bodie's heart to sink. 'My friend doesn't.'

'Ah, that's good,' Bodie said as, behind the truck, his team continued to hand the paintings up to Reilly, as if nothing untoward was happening.

'What is going on here?' the tall man asked. 'Kovacs said you had the wrong papers.'

Bodie nodded, still smiling. 'Is that what he meant? I wasn't sure.'

'There are a lot of you,' the tall man noticed.

'Many hands,' Bodie said. 'It's just easier work.'

'Can I see your papers?'

By now, the team had finished loading and was surreptitiously fanning out into more advantageous positions. Bodie was aware of their movements and now gestured at the cab. 'I'll get them for you. Maybe they gave me the wrong set.'

The tall man didn't comment. Bodie went to the front of the truck, opened the cab and looked inside. From here, he could see the top of the driver's head and his frightened eyes. Behind him, the tall man and Kovacs waited.

Bodie grabbed the sheaf, turned and handed them to the tall man. The guy spent a few minutes casting his eyes over them.

'You're not cleared for the house,' he said at length. He frowned at Bodie. 'What are you doing here?'

'I have my orders,' Bodie said. 'Could there be some mix up?'

Kovacs listened as the tall man explained what was going on. Bodie watched his team move into position. The tall man gestured at the truck.

'We will have to ask the boss. Wait here.'

Bodie wasn't about to let him go. At that moment, Kovacs gestured towards the back of the truck. The tall man turned to Bodie. 'He says he wants to look at the items you're loading.'

Bodie thought about that. Maybe it would be a good idea to get the men up into the back of the truck before dealing with them, or at least at the rear. It would make the fight less obvious. He nodded and waved a hand.

'After you.'

The two men started off, hands resting gently to the right of their holstered guns. Bodie walked directly behind them, and Cassidy drifted closer so that she was behind Kovacs. Reilly backed them up.

The men reached the back of the truck. Bodie attacked. He smashed a fist into the tall man's kidneys. Cassidy followed suit with Kovacs, hitting him on the side of the head with a hook punch. Both men folded under the unexpected blows, staggering. Bodie hooked an arm around the tall man's throat and hauled him backwards, squeezing hard. The man started to recover, sending a quick hand in search of his weapon.

Bodie had to readjust. He let go of the guy's throat and went for the gun hand, stopping it reaching the weapon and grabbing the wrist. He twisted. The men yelled. Bodie stepped around so that he was facing the man, taking the wrist with him and snapping it. This time, before the man could scream, Bodie clamped a hand over his mouth.

There was a muffled cry. Bodie let go of the wrist and drew the weapon. He aimed it at the man.

'Don't move,' he said.

Cassidy battered Kovacs around the head some more. The man flung both hands up to ward her off.

When he did, she kicked him in the crotch and then kneed him in the face. As he groaned in agony, she plucked the gun from his waist.

'Stay right there,' she said.

Neither man listened. Bodie's opponent flung himself forward head first, trying to land a headbutt. Bodie staggered away, keeping hold of the gun. The man overbalanced and landed on his knees, slapping his broken wrist on the floor. He opened his mouth to scream again.

Bodie smashed him in his teeth before he could utter a sound. Blood flew from mashed lips. The man groaned and went down hard, hitting the floor limply. Bodie rose to stand over him, still aiming the gun.

Cassidy sidestepped as Kovacs lunged at her. She left a foot behind, let him trip over it. The man face-planted on the gravel floor, moaning. Cassidy bent down to tap him on the back of the head with the gun.

'Not a word,' she said.

Kovacs lashed out at her, not understanding and certainly not getting the gravity of the situation. He tried to sit up, still lashing out. Cassidy sighed and then brought the gun crashing down on top of his head. Kovacs' eyes rolled up, and he collapsed, out cold. Cassidy shook her head at the limp form.

'They never learn,' she said.

Bodie kicked his opponent in the ribs. Not hard, just enough to make him take notice. 'Hey,' he said. 'Get up into the back of the truck.'

The man glared, but rose to his feet and started to stagger in the right direction. Jemma and Yasmine had been monitoring the perimeter just in case more guards turned up, but, so far, they were clear. Noises still came from the truck loading area by the winery.

Bodie helped lug the unconscious Kovacs into the back, then left Jemma and Reilly to truss the two men up with some of the equipment they'd bought from the hardware store. At this rate, they would have a truck full of tied captives. The job was completed with duct tape over their mouths, and then they were shoved into a corner. The tall man scowled at them, probably wondering how he would explain it to his bosses.

Bodie knew there was no time to waste. He slipped the gun into his waistband and then turned to the others. 'Let's grab the rest of the paintings,' he said. 'Yasmine, you stay up here to keep watch.'

The rest of the team ran with him.

CHAPTER FOURTEEN

Soon, they were back up the stairs with the last six paintings. Together, they loaded them carefully into the back of the truck, close to the others and away from the tied-up guards. Bodie was sweating profusely by the time they were finished. He jumped down and looked at the front of the truck.

'Right,' he said. 'Jump up into the back. I'm gonna drive us out of here back to the cars, and then you can get out. After that, follow me into the city and we'll leave this somewhere where the cops can easily find it. That sound good?'

They all nodded. Despite the mishaps with the guards, Bodie thought it had gone fairly well. As an afterthought, he asked Cassidy to join him in the front, just in case. They weren't out of danger yet.

Together, the two of them climbed into the front cab and got settled. Cassidy apologised to the bound driver for having to rest her feet across him. He didn't say a lot, just looked frightened. 'Don't worry,' she said. 'You'll be free to go soon.'

Bodie started up the vehicle. He was about to pull away when yet another guard sauntered out and passed across the front of their truck. The man had headphones in. Maybe he wouldn't even notice them…

The guard had almost passed them by when he glanced to his left, saw the truck, and met Bodie's eyes. His own eyes narrowed. He stared at the truck. Clearly, he could smell that something was off.

Bodie should have known there were just too many guards, and they were just too big of an object not to be noticed. They'd done alright so far, but maybe they had been extremely lucky. That luck appeared to be running out all too quickly.

The man held up a hand to stop them from moving. He rested his hand on the butt of his gun. Bodie's heart sank a little. If he asked to look around...

The man walked to the side of the truck. Bodie smiled and rolled the window down, keeping the engine running.

'*Kakpo pravis?*' The man asked.

Bodie nodded. 'Yes.'

The man shook his head. '*Kakpo pravis?*' he asked again. Bodie noted his hand was still resting atop his gun.

'Picking up a few bottles of wine.' Bodie said, not sure if the man spoke English, but taking no chances.

The man looked confused and shook his head. He backed away slightly. Bodie put all of his weight against the door.

'Come here, mate,' he beckoned the guy closer.

With a look of confusion, the guard took two steps forward. Bodie flicked the catch that opened his door and then thrust it hard at the man's head. The door smashed into his face, staggering him. Bodie jumped down from the cab and went after the guy.

The guard was no pushover. Blood streamed from his nose, and he was shaking his head in distress and shock, but his reactions were still swift. He reached for his gun.

Bodie was on him in a second, grabbing the gun arm and holding it pointed at the ground. The guy didn't let up an inch, using his free arm to punch Bodie in the ribs. Boie couldn't stop him – both his hands were concentrated on the gun.

Then Cassidy's feet hit the gravel at his back. She stepped around the struggling duo and lined up a devastating punch. The guard's eyes regarded her wildly. She was about to unleash when the gun went off.

The gunshot sounded devastatingly loud in the generally quiet area. Bodie's heart sank. It would attract a tonne of attention. Cassidy smashed the guard in the side of the head. He didn't go down, but pulled the trigger again. This time, Cassidy knocked him unconscious and watched him slither to the ground.

She grabbed his gun. Bodie leapt back up into the cab. He waited for Cassidy to climb into her side and then floored the accelerator. Grit and gravel flew from underneath the tyres. The engine roared.

Two more guards ran around the house and stopped in front of the truck. They saw their downed comrade and whipped their guns out of their holsters. Pointed them at the oncoming cab.

Bodie didn't slow. He kept his foot on the accelerator. He ducked as the men grew larger in the windscreen.

The men leapt out of the way at the last instant. They were almost too slow. The front of the truck clipped one of the men's fleeing legs, sending him tumbling and crashing into the side of the house. Cassidy yelled in the passenger seat. Bodie held onto the wheel as hard as he could.

The truck cleared the house and then turned right. The guards who had dived clear leapt to their feet and aimed again. But they didn't fire. Maybe they'd been told the cargo of these trucks was immensely valuable, Bodie didn't know, but they both stopped in place, then started running after the escaping truck.

Bodie held onto the wheel as the truck bounced and jounced across a couple of unexpected ruts. He winced as he thought about those in the back and imagined them hanging on to anything sturdy.

The truck roared past the front of the house with the two guards chasing. Out of the corner of his eye, Bodie saw the front door flung open and three more guards emerged. They looked shocked and were staring around wildly, as if perplexed. Clearly, this kind of thing never happened here.

Now there were five guards chasing them. Bodie found the driveway and flung the truck to the left, felt the tyres slew in the gravel. Again he spoke a silent apology to those in the back and then checked his rearview.

Three guards were still giving chase. Two others had broken off and were running for parked cars. Bodie swore.

'They're getting into cars,' he said.

'Step on it,' Cassidy shot back.

'I bloody am doing. It's not exactly a Ferrari.'

'No way are we going to reach the cars,' Cassidy said.

Bodie agreed. They wouldn't have enough time to switch people out, not with the cars giving chase. 'It's gonna get uncomfortable for those in the back,' he said.

'They can live with it.'

They would have to, Bodie thought as he mashed the accelerator pedal hard down. In the rearview, he could now see the woman he'd noticed on the phone earlier. She was shouting and waving her hands around as if giving orders. Maybe she was the one in charge.

The truck flew up the gravel driveway, heading for the wide open gates. Bodie hoped they wouldn't meet another truck coming the other way and his prayers were answered. Still, they had to slow as the drive took a sharp right and then an even sharper left.

The runners started catching up. They were waving their guns threateningly but had no intentions of using them. Bodie flung the truck right and then left and watched their progress in his side mirror. The lead runner was alongside the truck.

The gates were a few hundred yards away. Bodie came out of the sharp left and started to speed up. The guard was beside his door, shouting threateningly towards the window. He looked like he wanted to stop the truck with his bare hands.

'Sorry,' Bodie said. 'I'm not pulling over for you.'

He felt the tyres grip the gravel. They started to leave the runner behind. The gates loomed. Bodie aimed for the centre as he took another glance in the rearview mirror.

'They're coming,' he said.

'How the hell are we gonna outrun them in this thing?'

The simple answer was 'we're not,' but Bodie wasn't about to say it. He watched a silver and a red car set off in pursuit just as the truck approached the gates.

There was a truck pulling in through the gates.

His heart lurched. The truck driver saw him and hauled on. Brakes screeched. Bodie barrelled towards him. He didn't slow, *couldn't* slow. The incoming truck juddered as the brakes took hold. It was a quarter of a way through the gates and the gap it had left wasn't very sizeable.

Bodie aimed for it. He winced as he approached, seeing the gap wasn't big enough. The front of his truck struck the bumper of the other and shoved it slightly backwards, creating more space. Cassidy's side screeched down the front of the truck, snapping her wing mirror off and denting metal. There was a sound like thunder as metal struck metal, as things crumpled, but Bodie's momentum saw him through.

The truck bounced clear, emerging onto the main roadway. He flung the wheel to the right to stay on the tarmac.

'Where the hell are we going?' Cassidy shouted.

'The city,' Bodie said.

CHAPTER FIFTEEN

Bodie drove as fast as he could, flooring the accelerator. They flew past the space where their cars were hidden, unable to stop. The red car and the silver car were already in pursuit and coming fast. Bodie knew he had to stay ahead of them and that getting to the city fast was their only hope.

The truck flew past hedges and lines of trees, the blue skies unconcerned above. After a few minutes, they saw outlying buildings and then an industrial estate. The traffic grew heavier. Bodie came up behind a slow-moving tractor.

'Fuck it,' he said. 'Always a tractor in the way.'

The pursuing cars grew larger in the rearview mirror.

Bodie saw a gap in the oncoming traffic and used it to throw the truck out and pass the ambling tractor. Buildings now flew to both sides. Their pursuers got closer as they poured on the speed.

Bodie saw they were getting closer and closer to the city proper. The traffic thickened and now he couldn't go fast, but neither could his pursuers. The traffic was a great leveller. Nobody came to a standstill, but they definitely had to slow. Bodie watched as cars got between his truck and their pursuers.

'You think we can lose them in the city?' Cassidy asked.

Bodie shrugged. 'It's our only chance. We couldn't do anything in the open. What other option was there?'

'I was only asking.'

A sprawling fast-food restaurant appeared on the left. Bodie flung the truck into the car park, barrelled around it, and went out the other end, leaving via the entrance. The following cars were forced to do the same, losing ground as vehicles got in their way. Bodie found himself on a new road with a decent lead.

The road ran straight for at least a mile. Bodie flew past parked cars on both sides, going as fast as safety would allow. A car door opened in front of him. Bodie slammed on the brakes and narrowly avoided smashing it off. Their pursuers got closer.

They approached their first set of traffic lights. Bodie cursed. It was the one thing he hadn't thought of. The lights were currently at green but, in typical fashion, as they approached they started to turn red.

Bodie knew he couldn't stop. He flew out from behind the car in front, crossed lanes, and tore through the lights as they hit red. Horns blared. One car, coming in the other direction, had set off prematurely and now had to slam on the brakes, the car slewing across the road. Bodie's truck gently clipped the front end so that the other vehicle shuddered slightly and went on, racing across the junction.

His hope was that the following cars would be forced to stop. His heart fell when he saw them flung out of the queue by their drivers and then ploughing across the junction. They caused even more chaos, forcing cars to clip each other and run into the rear of others. The sound of rending metal filled the air. Horns sounded in Bodie's wake as he cleared the junction.

The red and silver cars kept on coming.

Bodie found himself rushing down another street. This one was narrower and had cars parked to just one side. When the pursuers started catching up, now right behind the truck, he knew he had to come up with something different.

It was risky, but he would have to do it.

He went faster. Cars sped towards him. At the last moment, he flicked the truck so that it leapt into their lane, causing them to jam on the brakes and turn the wheel. Then Bodie flicked the truck back to the right lane, leaving those behind him to deal with the oncoming car. The red car was forced to brake hard, the silver car almost smashing into it. Both cars ended up facing a different direction.

Bodie pressed on.

Now another idea occurred to him. It was desperate this time, but he thought it might work. Maintaining speed, he flicked the vehicle to the side, catching the back of some of the parked cars, but catching them only slightly, brushing them. This made some of them jerk forward into the car in front, but it also flicked their tails out. Two cars flipped right out, blocking the road.

Just what Bodie wanted.

The pursuers, already behind, lost even more ground as they met the new barricades. They couldn't easily get past the obstructions because of oncoming cars in the other lane. On the wind, Bodie now heard the sound of sirens.

'Shit, that ain't good.'

'They'll lock us up and throw away the key.'

'I know.'

It was time to end this, he thought. To escape the pursuit. Now was the best time. He took the next right, then a left, all the while going slightly faster than the speed limit, using every inch of the road that was available.

The red and silver cars were out of sight. Bodie looked to turn down as many random roads as possible, but was aware they weren't out of it yet. There were only so many roads available, and the pursuers would probably know them all.

'Do you have your phone on you?' he asked Cassidy. 'A route across the city would be nice.'

'I'm crap at sat nav stuff,' she said. 'But I'll try it.'

They were approaching a bridge. Bodie saw standing traffic on all sides. He was forced to slow and come to a halt as the traffic crawled across.

In the rearview, he saw the red and silver cars approaching. He bit his lower lip. 'Damn it. They're back.'

What next?

They crossed the bridge, blue water on both sides. At the far side, he saw a police car approaching, though the vehicle didn't appear to have any interest in him. He cringed as they passed, lights flashing, but didn't even get a glance from the officers inside.

Instead, they zeroed in on the red and silver cars.

Bodie almost cheered, but then felt horror as he saw armed men jumping out of the pursuing cars. They didn't hesitate to open fire on the cops, gunning them down in the street. Bodie saw bodies flying every which way, bullets colliding with flesh and the splash of blood. The guards showed no mercy, rushing right up to the police cars and opening fire into the windscreens. Then, they dragged the bodies out and shot the men in the head.

Within minutes, they were back in their cars.

'What's happening?' Cassidy asked.

Bodie swallowed drily. 'Those bastards just killed the cops. Shot them in cold blood. They're coming after us again now.'

With despair in his heart, he set off again, driving faster and faster. He pulled out in front of an oncoming car, made the guy swerve into a barrier. He took a right across the river and then looked for a quieter set of roads.

It seemed they had crossed a good deal of the city. Cassidy was struggling to follow her map app. Bodie found another road, several hundred yards in front of their pursuers.

'I'm pretty much out of ideas,' he admitted.

'We can't drive around forever,' Cassidy said.

'I know that.'

'No. What I mean is that we can confront them. We have guns, skills, man and woman power. We don't have to keep running.'

'But Cass, we're in the middle of a city. There could be casualties.'

'Then take us somewhere quieter.'

Bodie shrugged. If he knew the city that well, he wouldn't be driving around like a crazy person. He guided the truck left and right, maintaining a distance between himself and the cars. Twice he had to swerve a vehicle and was treated to a blaring horn. Once, those vehicles impeded his pursuers, which helped give him more of a lead.

The truck bounded down another narrow road, barely missing parked cars on both sides. Pedestrians gave it nasty looks as it barrelled by, clearly exceeding the speed limit. Bodie kept his eyes on the road.

A car pulled out right in front of him. Bodie didn't slow, just smashed right into its rear, tail lights and metal tearing away. The car flew to the left, getting out of his way. Bodie continued on, swearing, giving Cassidy a desperate look.

'This can't go on,' he said.

'I could lean out the window, loose off a few shots.'

Bodie thought about it. 'Keep them centred and well-aimed,' he said. 'Just give them something to think about.'

Cassidy unhooked her seatbelt and swivelled to lean out of the window. Bodie was forced to slow for several seconds, allowing the follow cars to catch up. As they did, Cassidy brought up the gun and fired.

Three bullets tore into the red car. Two smashed into the wings, but the third broke the windscreen, spider webbing it. The car veered to the left, smashed into a vehicle, and then righted itself. Something used their boots to smash the glass out, shards now flying everywhere.

Cassidy aimed again.

CHAPTER SIXTEEN

The sound of Cassidy firing filled the cabin.

Bodie concentrated on the road and the obstacles ahead. Twice he had to slow for ambling cars, bullying them out of the way and, once, nudging one aside. It was a fraught, strenuous, problematic ride, and it wasn't over yet.

Cassidy saw she'd damaged the red car, slowed it a little, and now focused her attention on the silver car. She aimed and fired, loosing off three shots. The bullets smacked into the car with resounding crunches, making the driver swerve and lose control. The car hit a parked vehicle and spun. The truck and the red car left it behind.

Bodie barrelled them along another narrow street. This time he ended up behind a truck, giving the red car plenty of time to catch up. He emerged into a wider thoroughfare, but the red car was right on their tail.

It got even closer. Cassidy, leaning out, fired another bullet. This time it clanged off an A-pillar, ricocheting into a nearby building. Bodie cringed and asked her to stop shooting.

'Too risky,' he said.

'Shit, what the hell are they doing?' Cassidy said.

The red car was as close as it could possibly get.

Bodie couldn't see it in the mirror. The only thing he had to rely on was Cassidy's commentary.

'There's a guy, the front seat passenger, and he's climbing along the front of the car, trying to reach for our back doors, I think. He's trying to get onto the truck!'

'Dammit.'

Bodie flung the vehicle left and right. He did not know if the manoeuvre worked. They ploughed down the wider street, enjoying the space for a while, travelling as fast as he dared.

And then he saw a flash of black.

It was in the side mirror. He narrowed his eyes and focused. There, in the mirror, he could see a black jacket. Someone was hanging onto the side of the truck and climbing forward, towards the doors. The man had made it.

'We've got company,' he said.

As he neared, Bodie saw that the man was holding on with both hands, sidestepping his way across a narrow side rail, gradually nearing the driver's door. He took his time. Bodie flung the vehicle to and fro, trying to shake him off.

'Sit back,' Cassidy said. 'When he appears, I'll shoot him.'

'Are you kidding? He'll be armed too. And I don't want you firing a bullet next to my nose.'

'I'm an excellent shot.' She sounded offended.

Bodie said nothing, but didn't sit back. The last thing he wanted was a bullet flying in front of his face. He watched as the man advanced, now halfway along the side of the truck. Soon, he would be level with Bodie's door.

He continued driving, keeping the vehicle

straight until the guy got used to it and then flinging it sideways. Once, the guy's feet flew off the ledge, but he grabbed hold of a top rail and reset himself. He was fearless, never stopping.

Bodie locked the door. The man's figure appeared on the other side. He leaned out, holding on with one hand now, and levelled a gun at Bodie's head.

'Stop!' he yelled in English. 'Stop, or I shoot!'

'If I die, you'll die too,' Bodie yelled back.

'Stop!' the man shouted again. Maybe it was all the English he knew.

Bodie ignored him. Seeing no reason why he shouldn't, he wound down the window, though. It was easier to reach the man.

'You want me to shoot the bastard now?' Cassidy asked.

'No, but you could show him your gun.'

Cassidy waved the weapon at the guy, who only responded with a deeper frown. Bodie kept the truck running at high speed. He could see the red car again now as it had backed off.

'Stop!' the man cried out.

Bodie took a hand off the wheel and punched out. His fist caught the hanging man across the jawbone, jolted his head back. He spat out blood and a tooth. Bodie didn't stop there. He kept punching, smashing the man across the face.

There was a loud gunshot. Bodie jerked spasmodically in shock. The truck slewed. A bullet flew right past Bodie's face. He could feel the heat. The bullet travelled at a thousand miles an hour, just inches from Cassidy's head, and exited through her open window.

Bodie exhaled. 'Shoot the bastard,' he said. 'Shoot the bastard now.'

Cassidy leaned forward, brought her gun up and fired in less than a second. The bullet took the man in the shoulder and brushed him off the side of the truck like a fly. He tumbled away, crashing into parked cars and coming to rest swatted on a front windscreen.

Bodie's heart continued to hammer. He tried a new move, trod hard down on the brakes. The red car didn't react fast enough. It smashed right into the back of them.

'Don't move,' Cassidy said.

Quickly, she jumped down from the truck. Bodie followed suit. Together they ran to the back, taking their guns out, and opened fire on the crashed car. Their bullets shattered windows and smashed through skulls. Blood tinted the inside of the car. Bodie fired eight shots, all of them hitting a target.

In the aftermath, there was a sudden silence. Bodie started walking back to the front of the truck.

The silver car roared up out of nowhere. Men jumped out, four of them, all with their weapons raised. They didn't hesitate to open fire, bullets slamming through the air. Bodie and Cassidy ducked behind the red car, staying low. After a few moments, Bodie rose, aimed the gun and fired. His bullet caught a man in the shoulder, sent him twirling around and then falling to the ground. To his left, Cassidy did the same.

And then the back doors of the truck opened and all the relic hunters jumped out.

Two of them were armed and leant their firepower to Bodie and Cassidy's. Hot lead laced the spaces between the two opponents. Bodie guessed there were only three enemies left now, and started to make his way towards them, pushing the advantage. Though they fought in the middle of a big city with houses and offices all around, they saw none of it, their focal point just the cars that formed their shields and the people they were fighting. Reilly pushed between two cars, coming around the red one, now just a few feet from their enemy. Jemma came in from the far left, trying to flank them. Bodie and Cassidy crept up the middle.

Another man popped his head up, firing. A bullet impacted against a wing mirror to the right of Bodie. The implement flew off in a cloud of metal and glass. Bodie didn't even have to look up; he just fired back and hit the man on the top of the head. There was a cloud of blood and then he disappeared.

Right then, the remaining two guards decided they had had enough and dived back into their car. One of them stepped on the accelerator and it flew backwards, trying to leave the scene. Bodie and Cassidy jumped on top of bonnets, aimed at the open windscreen, and fired. These men had tried to kill them and had killed cops. They might even still try to keep following until reinforcements arrived. They couldn't be allowed to escape.

Bullets ripped into them. The car drifted for a while, then swerved and hit a parked vehicle. The sudden silence was deafening.

Bodie turned to the others. 'Back in the truck,' he said. 'We're clear now. We have to get the hell out of here.'

Quickly, his companions turned and clambered

back into the truck. Bodie got a quick glimpse of the mayhem in there, scattered boxes and sheets and paintings everywhere. They were lucky no one had sustained an injury.

In the distance, he could hear sirens. People were standing in the street now the gunfire had stopped, some of them with their phones out. Bodie and Cassidy closed the rear of the truck and then climbed back up into the cab.

'Just drive,' Cassidy said quietly. 'Away from here.'

Bodie flicked the truck into gear and then drove off, leaving a scene of chaos behind. They needed to get lost, to find somewhere quiet where they could take stock. But first, the priority was to get away.

'Are you okay?' Bodie asked.

'There were a few close calls,' Cassidy said. 'But I'm fine. The guys who were trying to kill us – not so much.'

'I guess that means another gang's chasing us now,' Bodie said. 'As well as the Diablos, I mean.'

Cassidy turned to him. 'Not for long,' she said. 'All we have to do is figure out a way to turn the paintings over to the authorities.'

'It has to be done in the right way. It's a shame we don't have a contact.'

The traffic was thinning in front of him, so Bodie was able to make good progress. His heart still beating wildly, he searched for a place where they could stop and make plans and, somehow, extricate themselves from the mess they were in.

CHAPTER SEVENTEEN

Bodie let the driver go on a quiet boulevard and eventually stopped in the rear of a huge car park, behind a fast-food restaurant so that the others could escape the back of the truck and convene. They left the trussed up guards where they were and found a table that was relatively quiet. Around them, the bustle of the restaurant came and went, but the relic hunters were lost in their own world.

'We did it,' Lucie said as she munched a burger. 'We actually succeeded in what we were trying to do.'

Bodie could see the truck through a far window and nodded at it. 'All the paintings are inside and, I assume, undamaged?'

'We looked after them as best we could,' Jemma said. 'Not easy when you're slipping and sliding around the floor.'

'I can attest to that,' Yasmine showed off a few bruises.

'The paintings are fine,' Reilly said. 'The big question is: what do we do next? I mean, the Petrovs will be after us. The Diablos are already searching for us. And, let's be honest, we have a fortune in stolen art sitting in that truck.'

Bodie clammed up as someone walked close by.

'This isn't the place to discuss it properly,' he said. 'But I don't know where else we can go.'

'I do,' Lucie said. 'Give me ten minutes.'

They ate their meals and were soon ready to go. Lucie informed them she had booked them a temporary storage unit on an industrial estate about a ten-minute drive away. They could stash the truck inside and have a proper talk. Bodie nodded.

'That sounds perfect.'

Soon, they had left the guards behind in a tangle of arms and legs and were approaching the unit. The sun was going down. A blazing sunset lit the horizon as they pulled into the storage unit and locked the shutter door behind them. For the first time in hours, Bodie let out a breath of relief. They were safe. He looked around. The storage unit was compact and utilitarian, but it did have a small office on one side.

Yasmine was already at the door, opening it. Inside were three chairs and a large desk. The team filed in and closed the door, some sitting, others perching on the desk. They all looked at each other and, for a moment, nobody said a word.

'Back to the conversation,' Reilly said finally. 'What's the next step?'

'We could leave it here and phone in an anonymous tip,' Cassidy suggested.

'It needs to be more substantial than that,' Bodie said. 'We can't risk this haul flying under the radar. Don't forget, our initial plan was to find the treasure to get the Diablos off Reilly's back.'

'Well, now it's gone from one gang to two,' Cassidy said with a tight smile. 'And the Petrovs clearly don't care who they hurt. We're right in the middle.'

'Thirteen paintings,' Lucie said. 'Now wait a minute. Four are Rembrandts, right? And didn't you say the other nine were part of some ancient mystery?'

Reilly nodded. 'We should look at them.'

'Now wait a minute,' Bodie said. 'I don't think that's the point here. Ancient mystery or not, we can't just go off on a tangent.'

'Doesn't mean we can't take a look,' Lucie said. Her eyes were sparkling.

Bodie looked around the room. 'Does anyone else want to take a look?'

Yasmine nodded. 'I'm in,' she said. 'As well as burglary, it's what we do.'

Bodie laughed at that. 'I guess we did pull it off,' he said. 'Even after all these years. We've still got it.'

Cassidy looked nonplussed. 'I'd say we got caught, and we got damn lucky,' she said. 'They wouldn't have hesitated to kill us.'

Bodie sobered a little. 'Yeah, it was a close call.'

'What was the name of that painter?' Lucie said into the sombre silence.

'Gustave Auch,' Reilly said.

'So let's go look at some of Gustave's paintings,' Lucie said. 'See what jumps out.'

Since most of the team wanted to take a look, Bodie said nothing. He didn't see the point, but this was a democracy. He followed Lucie and Reilly out of the office and back to the truck, where they started to open the back doors. Yasmine turned on all the lights in the storage unit and then they were climbing up and headed toward the pile of paintings.

'One each, one at a time,' Reilly said. 'Let's do this carefully.'

They sorted the Rembrandts from the Auchs and brought the latter out of the truck and into the light. Lucie helped line them up along the back wall. Once they were done, the team stepped back to stare at the nine paintings.

'There appears to be three sets of three,' Reilly said, eyes narrowed. 'Do you see? Those three are similar in subject matter, then those three, and the final three.' He pointed at all of them. 'I think we should rearrange them in order.'

Bodie admitted he seemed to have a point. Several of the paintings definitely appeared to have a theme. He watched as the others walked forward, chose the paintings, and rearranged them. As they worked, he thought about the position they were in. With both the Diablos and the Petrovs after them, their options were limited. Their position was dire. But their plan had always been to hand the paintings over to the authorities. It was just a matter of finding the right way to do it.

He didn't like putting the entire team in so much trouble. Yes, they had to help Reilly – the guy had proven he was an important part of the team. But leading them from their relatively dull new life in New York, with all the decisions about what to do next looming, into such a dangerous mission? It didn't sit well with him.

The team had finished with the paintings now and all stepped back. Bodie saw three sets of three paintings, separated. The first set appeared to depict a ship somewhere in the Caribbean, with the first of the three being a closeup, showing all the intricate features of a ship's newly cleaned deck. The artwork was exquisite, making the deck stand out as if it was real. The second painting showed that same ship in all its glory, resting alongside a dock. Bodie was perturbed to see a man standing on the side of the dock – not because of the man himself, but because his head obscured the name of the ship. The third painting in the set showed the ship at berth, with a complex coastline behind and the shape of a town to its right.

'Interesting,' Reilly said, looking at the same set. 'I'm not sure what it's supposed to convey, though.'

Bodie was equally mystified. He turned his attention to the second set of three. This was an exquisite study of treasure. It depicted gold and silver coins, several large wooden chests and heaps of jewellery bearing some kind of seal. There were elaborate candlesticks, carven bowls and bright swords. Other weapons stood out too, including spears and shields. Whoever the horde belonged to was clearly some kind of warfaring nation.

Finally, Bodie's attention turned to the final set of three. The first was of a rugged coastline, the second a boiling sea, the third showed an underwater scene with a seemingly significant feature. The paintings were superb, but all in all they meant little to Bodie.

'I really don't understand,' he said. 'What's Gustave Auch trying to say with these?'

Lucie, in typical fashion, was still staring at the first set of three, taking in every detail. She was rapt with attention, her eyes wide.

'Aren't they great?' she said distractedly. 'See the brushwork, the sophistication. Auch was a talented painter, a maestro. But there's a lot to take in here. Possibly a whole story. We need an awful lot of time with them.'

'You called him a maestro,' Reilly said. 'Isn't that a conductor of an orchestra? A performer?'

'Yes, but a maestro is also a distinguished figure in any sphere. A genius. You've heard of a movie maestro? Well, Auch is a painting maestro.'

Bodie sighed. 'You mentioned time? That's exactly what we don't have.'

Lucie took her phone out and, carefully, began to snap pictures. She zoomed in on several aspects, taking more than one picture and, slowly, made her way past all nine. 'Now we have a record,' she said. 'But I want to study the originals for a while. At least give me tonight.'

Bodie looked at the others. 'What do we think?' He said. 'Shall we give Lucie tonight?'

'It can't hurt,' Yasmine said. 'We're well out of the way here. And I could do with a break after being flung around inside that truck today.'

'You should have been up front,' Cassidy muttered. 'Talk about being flung around.'

'Hey,' Bodie said light-heartedly. 'I hope you're not complaining about my driving.'

'Brings a new meaning to the words "fast and furious."'

Bodie huffed. 'We were being chased and shot at.'

'Being one of those in the back,' Heidi said. 'I have to say – your driving kind of sucked.'

Bodie let out a breath. 'Well, I thought you at least might have stood up for me.'

Cassidy let out a laugh. 'Bonking privileges doesn't get you total rights.'

Lucie, who hadn't heard a word of the conversation, fell to her knees in front of a painting, staring at it hard. When he saw that, Bodie knew what the answer to his question would be. They'd already lost Lucie to her research, and it wouldn't be a good idea to upset her. He looked at the battered truck and then the office.

'Might as well get comfortable,' he said.

'I, for one, am starving,' Cassidy said. 'I can't remember the last time I ate.'

Jemma whipped her phone out of her pocket. 'Problem solved,' she said.

'I ain't eating that.'

Jemma scrolled through the internet, searching for a takeaway. 'How about pizza?' she said.

Bodie settled in for a long night.

CHAPTER EIGHTEEN

Their pizzas arrived steaming hot and smelling divine. Bodie and Cassidy met the guy at the door, took the boxes off him and carried them into the room. Even Lucie turned her head when the aroma reached her nostrils.

The pizza guy had also brought alcohol in bottles. Bodie deposited them on the table along with paper cups and shuffled the pizza around so that they were easily accessible. Almost an hour had passed since the team had placed their order and they were all hungry.

They settled in and started eating, leaving Lucie to get on with her work. By now, the historian had also pulled out her phone and was looking up information as she examined the paintings.

'It's a good job she doesn't mind being left alone to work,' Cassidy said. 'Because if I'd waited any longer for food, I'd have passed out.'

Bodie took a huge bite of his triangular slice. 'Agreed,' he said. 'And the vodka's gonna help, too.'

They poured drinks and tried to relax. It had been a dangerous day with a lot of close calls, and they still weren't where they truly wanted to be. Reilly was still being hunted by the Diablos, and the Petrovs were undoubtedly out looking for them. But, for now at least, they felt safe.

'Thank God for pizza,' Cassidy said, devouring another slice. 'You know, all I wanna do tonight is get drunk.'

Bodie laughed. 'It does sound like a good idea.'

'No gangs. No paintings. No Diablos or Petrovs. Whilst we were lounging in New York, I thought I was missing the action. Now I'm not so sure.'

Bodie got up and poured her a glass of vodka and Pepsi Max. 'Have a drink on me,' he said.

They settled back and relaxed as Lucie worked. Eventually, the historian could bear it no longer and wandered in for a few slices of pizza, but she ate them very quickly and was soon back at her job. She didn't drink. She had an attentive look of concentration on her face that Bodie had missed.

'Dare I broach a potentially hazardous subject?' Heidi said when the pizza slices had almost vanished.

'Go for it,' Bodie said.

'Whilst in New York,' Heidi took a deep breath. 'It was obvious that we were all struggling with something. We have spare money now, enough to last us all a few years. But where do we go next? What do we do? That's the hard question. And I know you were all thinking about it. I just *know*. Does the team stay together, and if so, in what form?'

Her words created a vacuum in the room, as if all the air had been sucked out. Nobody looked at each other. Even Bodie paused with a drink halfway to his lips. There was a long silence.

And it was Heidi who had to break it. 'You see?' she said. 'The *hard* question.'

Cassidy, who'd had more alcohol than the rest of

them, eventually sighed loudly. 'I've been relic hunting with Bodie for more than half a decade,' she said. 'For years. Why would I want to change that?'

Jemma shifted in her seat. 'Me too,' she said. 'And Bodie, Cass and I have been together for more than a decade. I see no reason why that shouldn't continue.'

'It's never been a job before though,' Heidi pointed out. 'Not officially. You would actually have to work to find missions.'

Bodie hadn't said anything and wasn't sure he wanted to. He didn't like the fact that Heidi had brought this up now. It felt almost like a stealth attack.

'I've worked with you for a few years,' Yasmine said. 'Since Eli...died. I think I've found my niche in life. I'll happily continue.'

Only Reilly and Bodie hadn't commented yet. Another silence stretched around the table, this one slightly uncomfortable. In the end, it was Reilly who cleared his throat and spoke up first.

'I'm new to the team,' he said simply. 'I really have no say. But you guys have a special camaraderie and work together better than anyone I've ever known. It'd be a shame to split that up.'

Bodie watched as all eyes turned to him. He hadn't wanted to make this decision, and he certainly didn't want to make it now. But he couldn't remain silent forever. It wasn't fair to the rest of the team.

'Relic hunting has become our total lifestyle,' he said. 'It's what we do, and we're good at it. But do I want to form a company, a business, and run it whilst romping off all over the world looking for priceless artefacts? That's something I can't answer right now.'

Cassidy sipped her drink. 'But you must have a few thoughts.'

'A few,' he admitted. 'I don't wanna split the team up. I don't want to lose you, Cassidy, or you, Jemma, as we've been together forever. Don't know what I'd do without you. But the thought of turning what we do into a business...it doesn't feel right. I'm not entirely sure it's the right way to go.'

'How else could we do it?' Jemma asked. 'Go work for the CIA again?'

'I'm not sure they'd have us back,' Cassidy said with a grin. 'We wrecked a few things. Destroyed a few others.'

'Oh, I'm sure Pang would love to see us again,' Jemma said. 'We could re-ruin his life, and he'd deserve it.'

Bodie leaned forward. 'I certainly don't want to work for the CIA again,' he said. 'The way they treated us,' he shivered. 'That's not what I meant. And I realise jobs won't keep falling in our laps.' He glanced over at the paintings, thinking this one had done exactly that, but in a roundabout and precarious way. 'But do I want to do this for a living?' He shrugged. 'I don't know.'

'I do,' Cassidy said. 'I'd love to.'

There were similar declarations around the table, but Bodie wouldn't be moved. He held up a hand. 'I'm just saying how I feel,' he said. 'I need more time to think about it. I thought I *had* more time to think about it. There's a lot to unwrap.' He sat back, slumping, not quite sure where else to go with the conversation.

Now the silence had a slight edge to it. Bodie hadn't said what they wanted to hear, but he couldn't help that. He could only be honest and upfront with them. He would not rush into something he wasn't entirely certain about.

'What else would you do?' Cassidy asked him softly.

'Such a good question,' he nodded. 'What am I good at? Relic hunting and burglary. That's a tricky decision. But listen...I don't have to do anything, at least for a while. Maybe I want to enjoy the peace and quiet.'

The others didn't question him any further, respecting his decision. They went back to their drinks and what remained of the pizza until there were only a couple of thin crusts left. All the while, Lucie worked in the background, but now she consulted her phone more and more. Bodie wondered what she was researching.

'I find it funny,' Heidi said. 'That we have four Rembrandts in the back of that truck which must be worth a fortune, and no one's interested. We prefer our pizza.' She waved her half full glass of vodka, maybe a little inebriated.

Just at that moment, Lucie rose to her feet and dusted herself off. She took a last look along the row of paintings and snapped a few more photos. Then she turned and came into the office. There was an expectant look on her face, and a flush of excitement. She waited until the attention was focused on her.

'What have you found?' Jemma asked keenly.

'Gustave Auch,' she said. 'Was a maritime specialist. A great painter. As I said before, a maestro. He painted all manner of seagoing paintings. He was well known for his art even when he lived, and his pieces change hands for quite a pretty penny. The man lived a long time ago now, but his legacy lives on.'

'His legacy?' Yasmine asked.

'Like I said, he was famous. He's one of those painters that liked to put hidden meanings in his art. I guess now we'd call them "Easter eggs". Auch liked his codes and his secrets and almost every painting he ever did contained them.'

'And these nine?' Bodie asked.

'These nine are no different. They contain secrets.'

Bodie felt the old, familiar excitement stirring. 'And have you deciphered them?'

'No.'

Lucie's answer was so blunt he felt a moment of deflation. He hadn't expected that. 'Is it something we can work on?'

'I hope so. I need to talk to you about it.'

Lucie stood by the door, her phone in one hand, giving off those schoolteacher vibes. The entire room was focused on her.

'Are you ready for me to explain?' She said. 'That's good. Then listen.'

CHAPTER NINETEEN

Lucie held everyone's attention.

'According to my research, the maestro Gustave Auch painted nine paintings to hide some ancient maritime mystery. These are those nine paintings. Apart, they're useless to anyone wanting to solve the mystery. But together...that's a different story. Collectively, he called them his Royal Cycle, though I do not know why. The Royal Cycle travelled through some quite wealthy hands before ending up in that museum from where they were stolen, though nobody I think has chosen to keep up with the age-old mystery. Over the years, Auch has lost his renown, his name disappearing beneath the weight of more famous ones. For instance, the Rembrandts they resided with. I bet you guys thought the Rembrandts would be worth more.'

'They aren't?' Yasmine asked in shock.

'Monetary wise, maybe,' Lucie admitted. 'But the real wealth of the Auchs comes with the mystery they contain.'

'And do we have any idea what that is?' Bodie asked.

'I can break it down a bit,' Lucie said. 'And we can go from there. We know there are three sets of three, yes? Well, Auch wrote quite a few notes concerning the Royal Cycle, and they're published online if you look at the personal pages uploaded by his estate. There's a load of information there, some of it quite pertinent. Anyway, the first set of paintings answers one question, the second set another, and so on.'

Bodie frowned. 'I don't get it.'

'Okay, so the Royal Cycle tells of a great ship. A galleon. The first three paintings will reveal its name. The second set depicts the treasure it carried. And the third set will tell us its location.'

Bodie tried to take all that in. 'It's location?'

'Presumably the ship sank and Auch figured out where it went down.'

'And I assume it had a great treasure on board?' Reilly asked.

'All Auch said in his notes were unimaginable riches, a king's horde. That's it. The rest needs to be figured out.'

Bodie felt the pressure building. 'But we can't just go off on a wild treasure hunt,' he said. 'Not now. We're actively being hunted.'

'Well, I haven't figured it all out yet,' Lucie said. 'There's a lot more information to wring out of Auch's writings. And then I have to start working on the answer to the first painting. The name of the ship. Once we have that, the research should be easier.'

'And how do we do that?' Cassidy asked.

'The clues are in the first set of three paintings,' Lucie said with a shrug. 'They're all there.'

'I never noticed any.'

'I do recall the name of the ship being blocked out by someone's head,' Bodie said. 'Is that Auchs idea of a joke?'

'Could be,' Lucie said. 'He didn't even have to show the name at all. So yeah, it's probably an inside joke.'

'All I remember is a deck, a ship, and a berth,' Jemma said. 'Is that enough to figure out the name of a centuries old ship?'

'The clues are there for a reason, so yes. It will be. We just have to figure them out.'

The team glanced at one another. It was clear they all felt the anticipation building, the exhilaration of another treasure hunt. The thought of it overcame the problems associated with their current situation and made them smile.

'So where do we start?' Heidi asked.

'I told you. We figure out the name of the ship. That will lead us to the next clue, and so on. Who wants to help me with the first set of paintings?'

'Did you take plenty of pictures?' Bodie asked, seriously.

Lucie looked confused. 'Yeah, why?'

'Because I really think they should be loaded back into the truck,' he said. 'It's safer for everyone that way.'

Lucie turned to look at the long row of nine paintings. 'I guess so,' she said. 'It's not a problem.' There was a look of regret on her face, though.

'It makes sense,' Yasmine said. 'We're gonna be out of here first thing tomorrow. And then the cops will get them.'

The team wasted no time in rising and getting to work. Nobody wobbled too badly, so they hadn't had too much to drink. Bodie took his time, working slowly. The others went at their own pace. Soon, all nine paintings had been reloaded into the back of the van, and the team stood looking up at the truck.

Bodie closed the doors. Reilly sighed. 'Oh, I'm so looking forward to travelling in the back again,' he said. 'Can't wait.'

'It shouldn't be as bouncy as last time,' Bodie said.

Lucie was standing slightly apart from them, that same look of excited expectation in her face. 'Seriously, guys, we can't let this go. This is what we do. It's fallen right into our laps. We need to follow it up.'

'The treasure has waited for hundreds of years,' Bodie said. 'It can wait a little longer.'

Lucie shook her head. 'You don't know who's looking for it. A dozen unscrupulous types maybe. It could even be why the Petrovs stole it in the first place. To find the treasure. Maybe they're working on it right now. Or it could be the very reason the Diablos are showing a sudden interest.' She held out both arms. 'It's all possible, and we can't let them have it.'

'It doesn't upset our plans that much,' Cassidy admitted. 'We can still give the originals back to the police. Hopefully, they won't publish any photos for a while.'

'It's true someone could have got wind of the treasure,' Jemma said. 'And they're now seeking it. Today, it'll probably be worth a fortune.'

'And now, suddenly, we have a treasure hunt to think about,' Heidi said.

Lucie just grinned.

CHAPTER TWENTY

Bodie allowed that, since it was what they did as a team, they might be able to figure out a way to go after Lucie's treasure. But it would take some discussion, and some work. And there was the initial immense problem to confront.

What were they going to do with the paintings next?

'Can we do both?' he asked. 'Hand over the paintings and seek the treasure?'

'I don't see why not,' Lucie said. 'We have the photographs. We can sit down and research and work it out. I mean...we'd be doing the world a favour, right?'

'How do you work that out?' Cassidy asked.

'By stopping crooked, dishonest men and women getting to it first.'

'You actually believe our enemies are looking for the treasure?' Jemma asked.

'The Diablos suddenly developed a healthy interest in the paintings. The Petrovs stole it from them. I'd say chances are high.'

Bodie looked at Reilly, the real reason they were here, and studied his expectant face. 'You also want to go after the treasure?'

'I think it's the right thing to do.'

Bodie was about to discuss it deeper when a scraping sound caught his attention. They were currently standing in the warehouse, at the front of the truck, and the noise had come from just outside the roller shutter door. Cassidy heard it too and gave him a suspicious glance.

Bodie ran to the nearest window and looked outside. It was pitch black out there; the streetlamps doing little to illuminate the night, the vault above devoid of stars. He narrowed his eyes, looking for anything that might have made the scraping sound.

Down by the road, a few streets away, there were two parked cars. He was sure they hadn't been there before. Looking to his right, towards the roller shutter, he saw several slow-moving shadows.

'They've found us,' he said. He stared back at the truck. 'Maybe that damn thing has a tracker. But, whatever the reason, they're here. Outside.'

'Petrovs?' Lucie said.

'Yeah, that'd be my guess. We need to scatter. Meet back at the hotel in the morning.'

'I don't know about that,' Lucie tried not to look scared.

'You come with me,' Heidi said. 'But he's right. The more targets they have to chase, the better. It'll break them up. Now, move it.'

The team dispersed, heading for different exits. Bodie ran to the side door, along with Jemma. Heidi, Lucie and Reilly ran for the back. Cassidy and Yasmine headed for the stairs, aiming to go up. It was a mad rush, and amid it all, Bodie heard the roller shutter door shake. Their enemies were grouping outside.

Cassidy hit the stairs at a run, Yasmine a step

behind. They pounded up the concrete risers two at a time. At the top, a narrow walkway ran around to a mezzanine with boxes stacked high. Cassidy ran straight past the mezzanine, having spied her goal at the far end.

A door that led to the roof.

She'd not been idle earlier when they'd arrived at the warehouse. Cassidy was well-trained and knew to check her surroundings closely whenever she arrived at a new place. She already knew that the warehouses had been built close together and that the roof might provide the perfect getaway.

She raced for the far door. Below, the roller shutter door started to rise and two windows exploded inwards. She saw boots and arms and knew they were definitely under attack. As she approached the door, figures streamed into the warehouse. Most of them carried guns openly and, rather than enter the interior carefully as she would have done, came barging into the space without a care for their own personal safety.

She reached the door, Yasmine still right behind her. She reached out and yanked it open. The action caught a man's eye, and he started yelling and pointing at the two women. Instantly, three figures broke off from the group and started pounding up the stairs.

Cassidy exited the building and stepped out onto the roof. It was dark outside; the wind snapping at her hair. The flat roof stretched away in all directions, the area littered with debris and what looked like old, discarded machine parts. She quickly got her bearings and turned to Yasmine.

'Do as I do.'

The other woman nodded. Behind, the pursuers were reaching the top of the stairs. Clearly, they had their guns out and aimed because, at that moment, one of them started shooting.

Bullets ricocheted off the framework surrounding the door. Cassidy ducked and ran. It appeared capture wasn't an option anymore. From behind, now the shutter door was up, she heard the roar of the truck starting up. Was Bodie driving it out of there? The guy certainly had balls.

She raced across the roof, running for the eastern edge that she knew stood close to the next roof. Heaps of debris lay in the way, making her weave from side to side. She slipped on an old rotting newspaper but managed to catch herself before she fell. As she ran, she listened for their pursuers reaching the door.

It didn't take long, and they were noisy, yelling and shouting as if trying to reach her first. Maybe someone had put a reward on their heads. Another gunshot rang out in the night, the bullet not even coming close. Cassidy ran faster, moving as swiftly as she could through the perilous obstructions.

She leapt over a pile of rusted, tangled machinery, coming down hard on the other side. As she did, a bullet strafed the air where she'd just been, barely missing her. Yasmine was a few steps behind so hadn't made the leap yet, otherwise she'd have been shot in the back.

Cassidy approached the edge of the roof. There wasn't time to pause or to gauge the leap. She just had to trust to luck.

She reached the edge, got a quick look at a three-foot gap, a long dark drop, and the other roof and then leaped. As she did so, in midair, a bullet flashed past her head so close she heard the whine. It didn't put her off. She landed gracefully on the other side and then slowed a little, making sure Yasmine also made it safely across.

The other woman hit the roof at a run, almost overtaking Cassidy. Together, they'd done it. The new roof was slightly lower so offered a bit of protection. Cassidy made the best of it by pouring on as much speed as she was able to.

They raced across the new roof, not looking back.

'Stop!' A voice snarled from behind them.

Cassidy whirled in shock, still running. A short man had caught them up. He was bathed in sweat and his eyes were wide. He didn't carry a gun, or at least not openly. But he was right there, just steps behind. Cassidy saw the rest of their pursuers reaching the edge of the first roof and looking warily over the edge.

She took swift action. She stopped and turned fast, leading with her upraised leg. The spin kick caught the guy right across the face, snapping him sideways. He flew off his feet, rolling until he hit a pile of bricks. But he wasn't done, still sitting up and shaking his head. He reached into his jacket, found a knife.

And threw it.

Cassidy ducked out of the way at the last second, the blade slicing past her left ear, almost taking a chunk with it. The man leapt to his feet, drew another knife. Cassidy and Yasmine fanned out, waiting for him.

To their right, their pursuers were jumping across the narrow gap between roofs. They had no time to spare.

The man leapt at them, feigned throwing the

knife, and got closer. He thrust at Cassidy. She fought back fast and hard, grabbing his wrist and twisting it. The man gasped and kicked out, catching her shin.

Yasmine slammed him in the throat and then jabbed at his eyes, giving him something else to think about. The attack confused him, slowed him down. Cassidy swiped the knife from his grip, then stepped in with two knee-strikes, one to the groin and one to the nose. The man went down amid a spray of blood.

Cassidy picked up his knife and started off running again. She and Yasmine ran for the edge of the roof, seeing another narrow gap coming up. Behind, their pursuers were running again as they negotiated debris and piles of bricks and also tried to aim their weapons. Gunshots rang out, the bullets flying hopelessly wide because the shooters didn't stop to take aim.

Cassidy flew across the roof, running as fast as she dared. Halfway across, she saw a small pile of metal and couldn't stop. She ran harder, hurdled it, flying through the air. She stumbled on the other side, but managed to catch herself and saw the edge of the roof coming up ahead.

This time the gap was wider. Maybe five feet. She couldn't stop now. She reached roof's edge and leapt out across the empty space.

Came down hard on the other side. She checked back. The pursuers were coming more slowly, hoping they could pick off the fleeing women with their shots. It was a false hope – they just weren't good enough.

'There,' Cassidy spied something she needed to the right.

They ran in that direction. More bullets flew, going high and wide. Cassidy reached the northern edge of the roof and looked down.

'Fire escape?' Yasmine asked breathlessly.

'Let's hope the damn thing stays attached to the wall.'

Cassidy leapt onto it and started swiftly down the stairs. The metal rattled, but felt quite sturdy. She dashed down step after step, Yasmine right behind her, trying to reach the bottom before their pursuers reached the top.

They didn't quite make it. Cassidy was half a flight from the bottom when the men appeared at the top of the fire escape. Now, because they weren't running, they'd be able to aim better.

The bullets started to fly, clanging off the metal. Cassidy ducked as she ran, knowing it wouldn't help but doing it anyway. Yasmine yelped as a bullet flashed past her ear, burning it.

'That was too close!'

Cassidy leapt the rest of the way and then rolled, coming up on her knees. She took a quick stock of their situation. There was nobody around. Looking up, she saw two men crowded at the top of the fire escape, guns pointed.

'Move!' she yelled, scrambling out of the way.

The men opened fire. The bullets slammed between Cassidy and Yasmine, the gap a matter of inches. Cassidy would have preferred to take both men out of the attack permanently, but there was no chance of that.

For now, she would have to make do with escape.

Both she and Yasmine scurried into the pitch black night.

CHAPTER TWENTY ONE

Bodie fired up the truck and put his foot down. He had calculated that his surprise actions would earn him enough time to get away. The others had separated and run so quickly he only been able to invite Jemma along. Now, the truck was surrounded by the enemy and he had to act fast.

The truck lurched. It groaned and growled and grumbled. It juddered forward, still loaded with the art, and then headed for the open roller shutter door. The men in front thought first about their own safety rather than stopping it, diving and rolling out of the way.

Bodie hit the accelerator, and the truck rumbled through the door. Jemma held on tight in the passenger seat. He spun the wheel to the right, following the road. Men jumped up behind him, shouting and aiming their weapons. He concentrated on the road, expecting to come under fire at any second.

But no bullets came. It took Bodie a moment to realise the men must have been told not to fire on the truck for fear of damaging the paintings. Instead, they were running after it, putting away their guns and concentrating on their speed. Bodie counted four men in pursuit, slowly gaining ground.

'Faster!' Jemma shouted.

The truck was slow. It ground through the gears. Running men were already at its flanks, reaching out for some kind of support. Bodie gritted his teeth and urged the truck to get a damn move on.

It did. He turned right again, now on the road proper and passing by the gang's parked cars. One man grabbed a rail on the side and tried to haul himself up. As he did so, he slipped and fell, rolling right under the truck. Bodie winced as he felt the guy scrape the bottom of the truck.

The remaining three men slowed as soon as they reached their cars and jumped into one. Bodie saw the headlights come on, the car start to manoeuvre. He jammed his foot firmly down on the accelerator pedal and, just like before, found road after road, twisting and turning, trying to lose his pursuers.

Driving as hard as he could, he came across something that made him smile.

Ahead, he spied a truck park. There were hundreds of them all parked up in a vast area, all quieted down for the night. Bodie roared into the area, headed down a row and found a space near the end. Quickly, he turned the engine off and looked back the way he'd come. Jemma was silent in the passenger seat. The pursuing car hadn't been in sight when he made the move, so it could have no idea of where he'd gone. Even if the men guessed, they'd face a daunting task.

Bodie and Jemma waited, sitting and sweating nervously in the dark. The truck's engine ticked. He peered back the way he'd come, finally seeing headlights approaching. He held his breath.

The headlights veered away.

With only Jemma to see him, Bodie grinned.

***

Heidi, Lucie and Reilly burst out of the side door and looked wildly from side to side. They could hardly see in the dark after the bright lights of the warehouse and took a moment to let their eyes adjust. Heidi felt a little inebriated and knew she'd need all her wits to get them out of this.

She could hear sounds of pursuit.

The trio ran to the left, heading for more buildings where they might get lost. Heidi stopped and wedged a sharply angled stone under the door, hoping to slow down their pursuers. They raced with their heads down, keeping to the shadows.

Heidi pulled ahead, Reilly brought up the rear. The trio tore across a patch of grass and soon reached the next building, travelling along its side. As they did so, the door behind them burst open and three men practically fell out together. They looked up, searching for their quarry.

Heidi hugged the side of the dark building, heading around the back. The trio moved among the shadows, now staying as still as they could whilst moving. The men hadn't seen them, their eyes still adjusting to the dark.

Heidi reached the back of the warehouse. She slipped around and waited for Lucie and Reilly.

'They didn't see you?'

'No shooting,' Reilly said. 'So we're good.'

In the distance, they could hear gunshots, which seemed to come from above.

Heidi led the way down the rear of the warehouse. Soon, she reached the end and found a gap between that and the next one. She debated whether to hide in the gap or keep moving, decided to carry on. They needed as much space between themselves and their pursuers as possible.

There was a scuffle behind them. Heidi stopped moving and dropped into a crouch. She turned. Far back, in the shadows, she made out the three men – just figures peering around the corner. Holding her breath, she watched them.

'Hold it right there, you two!' One man shouted.

Reilly, on his stomach, slithered away into the gap between buildings.

The three men approached, guns out. As they got closer, they smiled, confident they'd cornered their prey.

'You can't get away from us,' the same man said, now grinning. Maybe he was the only one who could speak English. He turned to his colleagues and spoke in an unfamiliar language, making them laugh. Heidi and Lucie faced him defiantly.

'Don't make trouble,' the man said. 'Come with us now.' His accent was thick.

Heidi backed off. Lucie followed her lead. They had to make the men come forward so that Reilly could step out behind them. At the moment, they were level. If they looked to their right, they might even see Reilly's shadow.

'Stop moving.'

Heidi held up her hands this time, feigning compliance, and stepped back a little more. The men stepped forward, coming towards her. Their guns didn't waver.

'One more step and I shoot you in the leg,' the man said.

'Please no,' Heidi said quietly. 'We'll come with you. Just lower the weapons. Please.'

The man laughed, waving his gun in her face.

'You don't like this? I don't care. Now I want you to walk in front of us, back to the warehouse.'

Heidi didn't move. She wanted all of their attention on her. Now, she stepped a little closer because she knew Reilly couldn't take out three of them at once.

Reilly rose to his feet, an ascending shadow in the deeper dark.

Lucie stepped back again, almost hiding behind Heidi. A silent tension rose between everyone as each person waited for something to happen.

'Now,' the gang member said eventually, waving his gun. 'Walk past us.'

As he waved, Reilly struck. He kicked a gun from a man's hand, then looped an arm around the next man's neck as he grappled with his gun arm. The first man fell to his knees in shock and pain; the second lost vital seconds trying to figure out what was happening. Soon, his gun was on the floor and he was blacking out.

Heidi dealt with the third man – the English-speaking one. She lashed out, caught the gun, and sent it flying. The man made the mistake of ignoring her and trying to leap after it. She went after *him*, kicking him in the thigh and then punching him in the side of the head. He staggered, finally turning his attention to her.

Too late. She hit him head on, full in the face. She led with her elbows, first the left and then the right, connecting with his nose and jaw. Both broke, blood flew; the man fell to his knees. She followed that up with a knee to the side of the skull that sent his eyes rolling up into his head. He fell to the floor, twitching.

Reilly squeezed until his own opponent fell

unconscious. Just as that happened, the first man he'd attacked recovered and dived headlong for his gun.

Reilly couldn't reach him. He still had hold of the unconscious man and didn't have the time to stop him. Heidi was even further away, still kneeing her opponent in the side of the head. The first man reached for his gun, scooped it up and turned, hissing in anger.

The gun fired. The first bullet went into his own colleague, making him jerk. Reilly couldn't hold on to the dead weight. The man, the barrier, was slipping away. Another shot sounded. Another bullet slammed into Reilly's opponent.

Now the man paused. He turned his gun upon Heidi, started to squeeze the trigger.

And Lucie, ignored, forgotten, came out of nowhere. She ran hard and, albeit clumsily, jumped with her knees in front of her. She hit the gunman on the head, bowled him over. He groaned and fell, losing his grip on the gun. Lucie scrambled until her body was over it, shielding it.

Reilly threw the dead man to the floor and approached the shooter. He kicked him in the face until he fell unconscious, then whirled to Heidi.

'What do you say we get the hell out of here?'

Heidi nodded. 'Good plan, and...you two...thanks for the help.'

Lucie looked scared, but Reilly only grinned. 'Part of the team,' he said.

Lucie pulled herself shakily to her feet. 'That was...a first.'

'You're a natural,' Heidi said. 'Well done.'

Together, they vanished into the night.

CHAPTER TWENTY TWO

The team rendezvoused back at their hotel, Bodie parking the truck behind it and out of sight.

It was a battered, tired but upbeat group that met in the bar. They were all bruised and scuffed and dealing with unpleasant memories of their recent brush with death. They sat around a dark table in one corner and ordered much-needed drinks all round.

Bodie placed the keys to the truck on the table. 'Time to get rid, I think. We were lucky to get away from the warehouse. All of us.'

'Long past time,' Cassidy said.

'So we go with one of our initial plans,' Lucie said. 'Dump it somewhere and call the authorities.'

'But make sure the right people hear about it,' Bodie said. 'So the provenance of the paintings doesn't get lost. So it gets out on the news. And so both gangs hear all about it.'

'I've done some research,' Lucie said. 'When we're ready, I'll have someone to contact, as well as the cops.'

'The truck's dumped,' Bodie said, indicating the car park at the back of the hotel. 'It's as good a place as any.'

'You wanna call the cops now?' Jemma didn't

look happy as she sipped her double shot of vodka over ice.

'Are you kidding?' Bodie said with a grin. 'I want a good night's sleep first.'

The team smiled in relief, drank up, and filed off to their rooms. Bodie was asleep as soon as his head hit the pillow, Heidi at his side. By the time the morning dawned, they felt rested, took showers, and then went down for breakfast. Bodie thought it felt a bit odd – acting normal whilst having such a big secret parked just outside, waiting for them to unveil it. But they ate and then checked out and made their way to the airport.

Bodie then made the call to the authorities, revealing the location of the truck and its contents. Lucie made a couple of similar calls to dignitaries she thought would be interested in the find and would make a big deal of it.

Bodie then faced the rest of his team, sitting in an airport lounge. 'A job well done in the end,' he said. 'It didn't go as expected, but then nothing ever really does.'

'Hopefully the Petrovs will never find out who stole from them,' Yasmine said.

Bodie nodded. 'They shouldn't.' He then looked around, taking in the vast airy space of the airport. 'So the question is – where to next?'

Lucie perked up immediately. 'Anywhere,' she said. 'I know we have to leave Sofia, but it doesn't matter where we go.'

Bodie tried not to smile at her. 'And why's that?'

'Why? So that I can start the research into the treasure, of course.'

'Can't you do that here?' Cassidy asked. 'Save us a trip.'

Lucie shook her head. 'No, I need some peace, some time, and some quiet. I can't work properly in the middle of an airport.'

Bodie sat up. 'All right, then. Where do you wanna go?'

A chorus of city names sprang up around the table, some louder and more serious than others. Bodie was a bit nonplussed, but knew somebody had to decide on *something*. He heard Paris mentioned twice and came down on that. The team immediately bought tickets for the next flight to Paris, which lifted off in just over an hour, then sat back to wait. Bodie and Lucie kept their eyes on the news channels but, so far, nothing concerning the truck had emerged.

By the time they'd flown to Paris, landed, and found a suitable rustic hotel out of the city centre, there was still no news of newly discovered paintings coming out of Sofia. Bodie was disappointed. The sooner the news emerged, the sooner they'd get the two gangs off their backs. At least, that was the hope.

This time they settled down in the hotel's vast lobby, on plush leather chairs, and sat back, letting Lucie get stuck into her work. First, she brought up all the pictures again – the three sets of three – preparing to use them as prime reference material. Then she sat back, perusing the images.

'I've been thinking about this all the way here,' she said. 'How to go about it in the right way? I think I know the best way to go.'

Bodie sat back and watched her work, Heidi at his side. He felt relaxed, out of danger, out of the limelight. This was much better. He turned to Heidi and smiled.

'You happy?'

'I am now that we're not about to die.'

'I meant – in general.' He blinked.

'Yeah, I know. It's all a bit surreal at the moment. This new relationship.' She shook her head. 'It's fun, but where does it stand in the middle of a mission?'

Bodie hadn't thought about it that way. He wasn't quite sure what to say, so took his time. He glanced at his companions, saw them chatting easily to one another. Their lives were simpler now, at least.

'I dunno,' he admitted finally. 'We carry on as normally as possible, I guess.'

'Well, it's certainly different. I don't...I don't know how to proceed with it.'

Bodie shrugged. 'I suggest we go with the flow,' he said. 'And make the best of what we have. We could be thrust back into the action at any moment.'

Heidi grimaced. 'Let's not hope it's *that* soon,' she said. 'I need at least another two or three days of beauty sleep.'

Bodie carefully didn't respond to that. He watched Lucie work, took in the lobby's ambiance, sat back and drank coffee. Time passed. Lucie clicked away at her laptop, made notes, and frowned repeatedly.

Finally, though, she was ready to talk. 'You want to follow the next step in finding this treasure,' she said. 'Listen to me.'

CHAPTER TWENTY THREE

'What we have here is a splendid set of clues,' Lucie said, showing them the paintings. 'The first three, according to my research into Gustave Auch, reveal the name of the vessel we're looking for. Look closely. There's a painting of the ship, the deck, and a distinctive island. A jetty, if you will.'

'What do you make of it all?' Jemma asked.

'I'm using an app to match ships,' she said. 'Who would have thought such a thing existed? But I've run it twice, and nothing has showed up.' She looked disappointed. 'Which means the easy option is out of the window. I've trawled images for a while, looking for a match, but that's hopeless. There are too many. It'd be the luckiest find ever. There has to be another way to come up with the ship's name.'

'There are two more paintings,' Reilly pointed out.

'Exactly. The first is a closeup of the ship's deck, which reveals very little. I think it's supposed to be the first in the sequence – depicting only that what we're looking for is a ship. It's the third painting that's remarkable.'

All eyes turned to the third painting, which showed a ship at berth, a complicated coastline, and a sprawling town to the right. Bodie squinted, but couldn't see the name of the ship anywhere along its length. He shrugged. 'I don't get it. How is it a clue?'

Lucie tapped on her screen. 'It's not the ship at berth that's the clue. It's the surroundings. Don't you recognise the place?'

Bodie squinted. 'Not a clue.'

'And neither do I. But I think there's enough detail in the painting to tell us exactly where this is. You see the twisting coastline, the shape of the town, the two main recognisable streets?'

'But it's an old painting,' Yasmine said. 'The town will have changed.'

'I know that,' Lucie nodded. 'But there are plenty of images of towns how they used to be. We just have to find them.'

'Let's say you do that,' Heidi said. 'Let's say you narrow it down to the exact town. How will that help you identify the ship?'

'I'm glad you asked the million dollar question,' Lucie said. 'Because if we narrow it down to the town, we can find out exactly which ship used this berth and find out its name.'

Bodie thought about that. 'You can?' he asked.

'I'll have to trawl through some pretty old records,' Lucie said. 'But they exist. Do you see the writing in the bottom right-hand corner?'

Bodie squinted. 'It's a date,' he said.

'Another clue. So we know what era to check. The date is 1640. The first thing we need to do is identify the port.'

Bodie watched her work. Lucie had clearly already figured out exactly how to do it. She used her phone this time, importing the photographs into some advanced search engine and then clicking a button. The smile on Lucie's face was infectious.

Bodie sat back to wait. It was soothing, being able to work like this with no pressure and no bad guys sneaking up on them. Lucie clicked away at her phone and her laptop, and the others waited in anticipation.

Bodie surveyed the lobby as he waited. It was an engrained habit. Over the years, he'd found it imperative to always watch his back, and now he just couldn't shake the routine. So far, he'd seen nothing untoward though he was still aware of the valet standing surreptitiously in one corner, the guy at the reception desk almost certainly carrying a concealed weapon and the woman seated eight feet away who'd been on her phone constantly for the last hour leading some kind of online business meeting. He was aware of people coming and going, the staff and two managers he'd seen and even knew their names. Bodie found he was on high alert even when he was supposedly slacking off.

Lucie blinked as her phone dinged. She looked down, her eyes widening. 'I've narrowed it down to three potential sites,' she said. 'I now just have to trawl old records to match the town.' She started tapping away on her computer, bringing up old images. Some were speculation or fantasy, others far more serious depictions of what a town might have looked like in the seventeenth century. Lucie concentrated her attention on those.

'I'm liking this,' she said, showing them a painting of a town that looked very similar to the one Gustave Auch had done. The streets were the same shape, the distinctive buildings almost identical. The size of it looked similar and both main streets were alike. Bodie saw no obvious dissimilarities.

'A shame we can't see the coastline too,' he said.

'That'd be too much to ask for. But if we decide on a town, we can check the coastline too. I think this matches.'

Bodie studied it closely. 'The church steeple is the same. The triangular shaped structure there – it's almost a duplicate. And the shape overall is almost indistinguishable. I hope this is a port.'

'One of the most important of it's time,' Lucie said. 'It's Nassau.'

Bodie was impressed. 'That's perfect then. In the seventeenth century Nassau was one of the most significant ports in the world.'

'It wasn't even called Nassau until the late seventeenth century,' Lucie said. 'But pirates such as Blackbeard, Jack Rackham and Hornigold used the island as a base. Any ship berthing there must have been extremely well guarded.'

'Are there records dating that far back?' Jemma wondered.

'Where do you think the pirate stories came from? There are plenty of documented stories. There are accounts, and drawings and pictures,' Lucie said, delving deeper. 'Now that we've identified Nassau, we can dig into those.'

'I'll check the coastline just in case,' Jemma said, also clicking away.

Bodie let them work. Again, he reconnoitred the lobby, seeing the same people and new ones, assessing. He saw no threats. In addition, Cassidy was also on lookout and, twice, had sauntered off to take a good look at the perimeter, including the outside of their hotel. Each time, she had returned with a satisfied smile.

Bodie took the time to check the news once more. This time, on checking Sofia's local news, he got a result.

'It's up,' he said. 'The news has broken. Sofia's press is reporting the discovery of millions of dollars of stolen art. It'll be worldwide coverage soon. We can't ask for more than that.'

He watched a report that detailed the location and finding of the truck, its back thrown open so you could just glimpse the wonders inside. Soon, the report showed paintings being removed from the van and transferred carefully to another. Bodie kept watching, listening for something in particular.

Soon, he heard it. It seemed information about the vehicle had come from an anonymous source. Bodie smiled. He liked that. The reporter went on to say they did not know who had called in the find, but that the authorities were grateful the lost art had been recovered. Nothing else was said about the mysterious caller.

Bodie grinned at his friends. 'Looks like it worked, folks.'

They congratulated themselves as Lucie continued to work. Now, it seemed, they were off the hook. Reilly, too, was in the clear. Of course, there was always the chance the Diablos could take offence and maintain their search for him as some kind of vendetta. Bodie hoped that wouldn't be the case.

And now the Petrovs, too, had nothing and no one to chase. Maybe they'd even blame the Diablos.

Bodie turned his attention to Lucie as she started to speak.

'There are quite a few dusty old accounts of the ships that used to make berth at Nassau. Many dates, many ships. I'm reading old tales, old records, statements. Some official documents too. There are descriptions and even a few drawings linked to the records. I've even found an old maritime artist who used to draw the ships at anchor and then write down what he liked about them, what he observed. He's dated his work and, here, we have 1640. There are five ships related to that date.' She squinted at the screen. 'And I think he's drawn the ships in good enough detail for me to tell them apart.'

'Can you compare them to our ship?' Yasmine asked.

'Oh, yes, easily. There's quite an obvious match.'

Bodie realised Lucie had already made the connection. She was smiling, her eyes bright. Now she sat back and turned her laptop around.

'Do you see?'

Bodie leaned forward, as did the others. He saw four different drawings on the laptop screen, all dark pencil and shaded areas. The masts were depicted in great detail, clearly the primary interest of the artist. And it was the masts that distinguished them.

Bodie took in the photograph of their ship with its name obscured. Now he studied the drawings, searching for the correct ship.

It practically jumped off the page. 'There,' he tapped at the third image. 'That's it, no doubt.'

The others concurred. Lucie enlarged the image so that they could all read the name on the side of the ship.

'The Lady Royal,' Reilly said.

CHAPTER TWENTY FOUR

'What do we know of the Lady Royal?' Bodie asked.

'Nothing yet,' Lucie said. 'But give me some time.'

'We know something,' Reilly said. 'If you now move on to the second set of three paintings...'

Bodie waited for Lucie to load them up and show them around. He saw immediately what Reilly was getting at. 'The loot,' he said. 'We know that the Lady Royal carried a lot of loot.' He stared at the second set of three paintings harder, taking in the gold and the silver, the diamonds and the rubies. It was a fantastic haul.

Bodie suddenly thought of a question. He turned to Reilly. 'After you stole the art, did you take any photos?'

Reilly ground his teeth. 'Yeah, the guys took loads. No doubt they all ended up back at Diablo HQ.'

'Which means they could start searching for the same treasure at any time.'

'I guess so. If they think about researching Gustave Auch, that is.'

'Why would they?' Cassidy shrugged. 'They're a criminal gang.'

'But not all braindead assholes,' Reilly said. 'There were some clever people in there. Some who could definitely make the connection and might think it worth it to do a little research. Especially to find out the worth of the paintings. And that would lead them straight to Auch and the info *we* learned about him.'

Bodie kept his silence and went up to the bar to order another coffee. They couldn't second guess what the Diablos or the Petrovs would do. Of course, the Petrovs could have photographed the paintings too – they might already know about Auch and the treasure, might be researching it even now. Both gangs might. Which put a serious question mark over the entire mission.

Given time, he knew, the authorities would discover the information too.

Which suddenly put an urgency in his mind. This last few hours of soothing inactivity had been good. He should have known it wouldn't last. He returned to the table, now bristling a little with tension.

'We need to ramp this up a bit,' he said. 'For all we know, the Diablos, the Petrovs, and soon the authorities could be doing the same thing we are. If we want to get there first, unchallenged, we should hurry.'

'Agreed,' Lucie said. 'Because my research is...incredible. You won't believe what I've found.'

Bodie sat down again. 'Tell us.'

'The Lady Royal was filled to the gunwales with a vast treasure. Sent by a king of Spain to appease some traitor in England, it was known widely as the El Dorado of the Seas. Now, as you might know, El Dorado itself was first reported in the sixteenth and seventeenth centuries and was supposed to be somewhere in South America. The city of gold. But this ship...it earned its nickname because of the massive wealth it carried.'

'The treasure must be...enormous,' Jemma said.

'To earn the nickname El Dorado of the Seas in the seventeenth century, I'd say immeasurable,' Lucie said. 'Imagine what it'd be worth now.'

Bodie stared at the wealth portrayed in the paintings. Lucie's words were evoking a deep emotion in his soul. 'It's incredible,' he said.

'We already knew the treasure was huge, but not this big,' Cassidy said. 'Perhaps we should let the authorities handle it after all.'

'But what if the gangs are already searching for it?' Reilly said. 'We can't allow them to take it. The wealth will make them unstoppable.'

Bodie thought that was a good point, and his hungry inner compass was already focusing on finding the treasure. He just couldn't help it.

'Do you have any more information?' he asked Lucie.

'Of course. It's me. Now that we know the name of the ship, the information is plentiful. The Lady Royal sailed in 1640 and then again in 1641. It was lost during 1641 with this incredible treasure aboard. Apparently, it was forced to set sail at the wrong time of year and hit some dreadful weather along the way. At some point, it sank and disappeared forever. Of course, nobody knows how. Could have been a hurricane. A rocky coast. A cliff. Saboteurs. Or even pirates. Either way, the Lady Royal never made it to its port and was never seen again. Of course, someone must have seen it go down because that someone told where it was.'

'Is there any kind of inventory of goods?' Jemma asked.

'A brief, rough overview. One of the most famous items was the sword of the king himself. Called the Tazona. There were several jewels from the Queen's collection, even some of her wedding gifts. There was also a diamond known to be one of the largest in the world at the time.'

'And why would a king of Spain send so much wealth to appease this traitor?' Heidi asked.

'Apparently, he would be instrumental in the downfall of the English hierarchy,' Lucie said. 'It was worth the investment.'

'Until it all went wrong,' Cassidy said. 'What else was on board?'

Lucie scrolled through her computer. 'All manner of jewels. Necklaces. Crowns. Rings and bracelets. Even clothing – some of the best fashion pieces of the time. And then the goblets, the plates and other pottery. Another large draw were the weapons — the swords, the lances, the shields. All Spanish made and considered cherished pieces. You're talking a snapshot of the wealth of an entire nation. The king really went all out to appease this traitor.'

'Quite the haul,' Bodie said. 'If you can find it.'

'All the bad guys need is the name of the ship,' Lucie fretted. 'Then the rest of the information can be found online. What happened, what was on board. The circumstances of the voyage. Everything.'

'And the name of the traitor,' Bodie said, reading. 'I wonder what happened to him?'

'Doesn't matter now,' Reilly said. 'What matters

most is that my old crew might have the same information that we do. They may say they want the paintings back for their nett worth, but maybe there's an ulterior motive.'

Bodie was feeling more urgent with every passing second. 'We know the name of the ship,' he said. 'We know what she carried. All we need now is the location.' He turned to Lucie. 'Do you think you can tell us that?'

Lucie looked excited. 'It's next on the agenda. But what the hell are we gonna do if we get there and see two gangs fighting over it?'

Bodie had already thought that far ahead and opened his mouth to answer, but Cassidy got in first. 'We join the fight,' she said, only half joking.

'We're relic hunters,' Bodie said. 'This is what we do. I'm sure we can beat a bunch of bad guys to that treasure.'

'Then let's get started,' Lucie cracked her knuckles and turned back to the computer and its images. 'I'll move on to the third set of paintings.'

Heidi nudged Bodie's leg. 'Ya think this is gonna come down to a fight?'

He shook his head. 'Nah, of course not. I think we're giving the gangs too much credit. They won't be following the same clues. Not a chance.'

He smiled and turned away, wishing his words were reflected by his heart.

CHAPTER TWENTY FIVE

Lucie worked fast and hard, employing every trick in the book. She worked the computer and her smartphone in tandem, managing the laptop at the same time as trawling through a search engine for information. She turned up volumes, but most of it was useless.

Bodie ordered more coffee, having lost count of how many cups he'd had already. The team ordered lunch served at their table too, wasting no opportunity to get some food inside them. It was a pleasant, though boring few hours as they waited for Lucie to finish up her task.

Bodie was just fitting a small chunk of steak into his mouth when Lucie looked at him speculatively. He knew that look.

'What have you found?'

'The first of the paintings shows a rugged coastline. Could be anywhere in the world, but again, it's very detailed. I could have matched it with a terrain app, I think, but I don't have to.'

He stared at her. 'Go on.'

'I continued researching the Lady Royal at the same time as the paintings. There's a trove of information on there and, one line, close to the end, tells us that the Lady Royal went down off the coast of Cornwall.'

Bodie couldn't help but smile. 'Nice,' he said. 'That narrows it down.'

'To confirm, I ran the coastline painting through a map app, one of those coastline recognition thingies. It matches almost perfectly.'

'Cornwall?' Bodie reaffirmed. 'I guess it makes sense if they were sailing to appease some English traitor. They almost reached their goal.'

'So close,' Lucie said. 'The receipt of such a treasure could have changed everything back then.'

Bodie didn't want to dwell on that. 'So we know it went down off the coast of Cornwall,' he said. 'What's next?'

'Narrowing it down.' Lucie kept working. She turned to the second painting in the set and turned her laptop around so that they all could see. Bodie studied it.

'Basically, it's telling us that the ship sank,' he said finally. 'That it's at the bottom of the sea.'

Lucie nodded. The painting was an underwater study of the same ship they'd seen in the early paintings. The mast was purposely intact. Bodie saw a large ship with no name – a sprawling, impressive galleon – surrounded by the fauna of the sea. He saw rocks and algae through a shimmering haze, all the colours dulled by the sea. It was a remarkable study.

'I guess that's its ultimate resting place,' Yasmine said.

'Yeah, I think that's the point of the painting,' Lucie affirmed. 'To acknowledge the sinking of the ship,' she took a breath. 'Which leaves just one painting.' She turned the laptop back around.

Bodie watched her work. The researcher's eyes

never stopped flicking between screens and across the paintings. This time, though, it didn't take her long to announce her findings.

'It's pretty straightforward,' she said.

'Even Reilly could get it,' Cassidy said with a grin.

'Hey,' Reilly said. 'What did I do to deserve that?'

Cassidy patted his shoulder. 'You're just being you,' she said.

Reilly tried to look affronted, but failed. It was all about being part of the team. Bodie leaned forward to catch Lucie's attention.

'What do you have?'

Again, she turned the laptop towards them. 'Take a look at the third painting.'

Bodie did so. This time, the canvas portrayed the enormous galleon once again at the bottom of the sea. It lay intact, upright, with its mast looking perfect. If it wasn't for the obvious underwater effects, it could almost be sailing on the high seas. But the ship wasn't the only feature.

'What's that?' Heidi asked, craning her neck to see.

Bodie examined it. 'An oddly shaped, large rock,' he said. 'Are you saying that this is an underwater feature and will pinpoint the position of the wreck?'

Lucie nodded. 'That's exactly what I'm saying. Auch has painted the rock in relation to the ship. Essentially, it's a marker.'

'And all we have to do is find the marker,' Bodie said, thinking hard. 'Are there sites that map the bottom of the sea?'

Lucie held up her phone. 'Already on it. I don't know how accurate the painting is, but the rock is pretty prominent.'

'I don't get it,' Reilly said with a frown. 'How could Gustave Auch have known exactly where the ship went down, and how could he know about this rock?'

'My thoughts exactly,' Lucie said. 'And the only thing I can come up with — survivors. It can't be that deep. Maybe it sank in shallow-ish water. The survivors swam away from the wreck and made it to shore, shared their accounts later. Auch did his research and believed what they were saying. And then – he came up with this series of paintings.'

'So it's speculation based on centuries old accounts?' Bodie said.

'Isn't all relic hunting?'

Bodie blinked at that. 'I guess it is,' he said.

Lucie tapped the image of the rock on the screen. 'This narrows it down to the exact spot. If we can map this, find out where it is on the seabed, we can sail right to the location of the wreck. We'd be right over the top of it!'

'If Auch's information is accurate,' Heidi said, taking Bodie's side.

Lucie shrugged. 'We haven't carried out an operation yet where the information has been entirely accurate. We rely on old accounts.'

Bodie thought about it and had to agree. Lucie was right. The very act of relic hunting put you reliant on some age-old account and the fact that they were telling the truth, that they weren't being bamboozled, that they at least had an idea of what they were doing. How was Gustave Auch's painting cycle any different?

'This feature,' Lucie said. 'I've already mapped it.'

Bodie was surprised. 'It's that easy?'

'There are only so many sites you can use. And once you've inlaid the image, it doesn't take long. Thankfully, Auch is a master painter. Did you know that? Gustave Auch is acknowledged as one of the old masters?'

Bodie didn't, but that was far from the point of the conversation. 'Wait,' he said. 'The rock feature has been mapped?'

'Yes, probably through satellite scans of the area. They make the scans and then put them online, just like Google Maps. The lucky breakthrough is that Auch painted such an excellent likeness.'

'I'm not sure that's luck,' Jemma said. 'Auch appears to be way ahead of his time.'

'You're probably right. Either way, we should gear up to head for Cornwall.'

Bodie heard the excitement in her voice, the anticipation. Were they really about to embark upon another relic hunt? It had been a while.

'All right,' he said. 'Let's do that.'

CHAPTER TWENTY SIX

They travelled to Heathrow and then hired a car to drive to Cornwall. Bodie was at the wheel, and didn't hang around, driving at the speed limit the entire way. At first, the London traffic bogged them down, but then the road opened up for a bit until it became single lane roads with high hedges and few views. If they got stuck behind a slower vehicle here, they were there until the person turned off.

The trip to Cornwall took them around four hours. By then, it was evening, and they were forced to look for a hotel. Lucie found them a place close to where they needed to be and booked them in so that when they arrived, they could head straight up to their rooms. Bodie and Heidi shared one whilst the others all went separately. They followed the usual routine of resting, eating, and then sleeping, getting ready for the morning.

The next day, they met at breakfast.

Lucie led the conversation. 'The good news is that there's a cliff near here where, if there's no fog, we can look out over the sea and spot the exact place we want to be.'

'You have the GPS coordinates?' Reilly asked.

'Yes, I have those too. But I think a reccy from the cliff would be the best place to start.'

Bodie thought she was probably right. The team finished their breakfast and then walked to their outsized car before heading out into the day. It was bright and clear outside, the perfect kind of day for sightseeing. Bodie followed Lucie's directions and soon they were pulling into a small parking area that overlooked the English Channel. Lucie assured them it was the right position.

They filed out of the car. A fresh breeze struck them in the face, carrying with it the salty tang of the sea. Bodie felt a little spray sting his eyes and kept his face down, studying the rocky, gravel-strewn ground. The team crunched their way over to the cliff edge.

Bodie raised his eyes and looked up. It was a beautiful sight; the sea stretching away for as far as his gaze could reach, glimmering where the sun touched the tops of the gentle waves. It was vast, endless, mesmerising. Bodie looked from horizon to horizon, trying to take it all in.

The others, at his side, were equally silent as they studied the vista. Standing here, looking out, reminded Bodie of a time they'd stood at the edge of the Grand Canyon in the US, just before meeting another world-class team.

'Obviously, from up here, I can't pinpoint the exact location of the ship,' Lucie said softly. 'But I don't like the look of that.'

Bodie refined his vision. He looked closer to the cliff, maybe a few miles to the south. What he saw made his heart race.

'A ship,' he said. 'At anchor.'

'I can't be certain that's our spot,' Lucie said. 'But it's pretty damn close.'

Bodie felt helpless. He turned around. 'Right,' he said. 'The first thing we need to do is go get supplies.'

They walked away from the cliff and drove to a nearby supply store where they stocked up on everything they thought they might need. It was a specialist shop and sold and rented a wealth of stock. Bodie and the others rented diving suits and tanks and face masks. They bought binoculars and flashlights, an altimeter and much more. Bodie helped load all the new gear into the back of the car and then they returned to the cliff site.

'Right,' he said. 'Let's take a look.'

They had two pairs of binoculars. Bodie raised one up and fixed them to his eyes. He focused on the faraway ship and zoomed in, trying to see any activity on the deck. It was some kind of trawler, a big one, probably rented from a nearby dock. Bodie watched the decks closely.

Beside him, Reilly also fixed a pair of binoculars to his eyes, keen to eyeball the trawler.

Bodie saw nothing at first, no men, just a few unclear figures in the cabin. He kept looking. After a while, someone came out on deck. His heart skipped a beat.

They were wearing a diving suit.

'You see that?' Reilly asked.

'Yeah.'

The man was wearing a diving mask, so couldn't be recognised. As Bodie watched, another man came up behind him. This guy was also wearing a diving suit, but his face was uncovered.

Bodie looked at Reilly. 'Hope you don't recognise him.'

'I don't.'

They continued to watch, satisfied that the trawler was far enough away that the people on board wouldn't notice them unless they too used field glasses. But, hopefully, they would have no reason to. Bodie scanned the deck, monitoring the divers.

'What do you think they're doing?' Heidi asked.

'It's very close to where I would imagine the Lady Royal is,' Lucie fretted. 'Very close.'

'We won't know for certain until we get out on the water,' Jemma said.

'Is that a police vessel?' Yasmine suddenly asked.

Bodie put the binocs down. He'd been so focused on the ship he hadn't seen the bigger picture. Now, he saw a white boat cutting through the seas, bouncing on the waves. It approached the trawler, then gave it a wide berth, moving away. Bodie narrowed his eyes, thinking hard.

'Either they have permission or they aren't doing anything illegal,' he said. 'I don't know where the law stands. To all intents and purposes, the trawler is just chilling.'

'I don't think there're any restrictions around here on "chilling",' Lucie said. 'When I looked into it, there's no obvious law against diving. I'm not sure how that changes if you actually find something.'

'That's when the government steps in,' Cassidy said. 'When there might be some wealth attached to it.'

'That's when every government steps in,' Bodie said. 'Greedy little bastards.'

'Oh, shit,' Reilly suddenly said. 'Crap.'

The man still had the binocs glued to his eyes. Bodie raised his own, focused on the trawler. 'What do you see?'

'Fucking Marco.'

'A what?'

'It's fucking Marco. I don't believe it.'

Bodie focused on a new diver. This one was visibly overweight, barely fitting into his suit, and had a black, bushy beard. He carried his mask in one hand and an air tank in the other and he looked none too pleased.

'You're saying you know that dude?'

Reilly nodded. 'Yeah, he's a lieutenant in the Diablos. A real nasty one. He's been with the gang forever, though I've never seen him dive before. The other two must be professionals they've drafted in and Marco is accompanying them.'

At that moment, another figure appeared, this one also carrying an air tank. Reilly drew in another chunk of air. 'Shit, that's D'Angelo. Yeah, the gang's all here.'

Bodie grimaced and turned to Lucie. 'The news couldn't be much worse,' he said. 'They beat us to it.'

Out on the water, the police ship again cruised by, showing little interest in the trawler. But its presence pleased Bodie. The proximity of the police would dilute any violent responses the Diablos might have.

Bodie watched as the divers got themselves into position at the side of the ship. Now, others came to join them, and Reilly was naming name after name.

'It's a who's who of the Diablos,' he said. 'The only person I can't see is the big boss. He's probably too important to make the trip.'

'So what do we do now?' Lucie asked. 'They clearly beat us to it.'

Bodie watched closely. 'They're not armed,' he said. 'At least not openly. We're in the UK, so firearms are illegal. Of course, that doesn't mean they can't get them. But with that police boat patrolling regularly and potentially other eyes on them, I don't think they will risk it.'

'Which means?'

Bodie grinned. 'A good bit of healthy competition.'

Reilly's mouth dropped open. 'Are you kidding? That's the Diablos.'

Bodie counted. 'I see six of them. Maybe a driver too. We have the same number of people. They couldn't overpower us, and my guess is they won't even try. We park up close by and do our thing.'

'Park up?' Cassidy said sarcastically. 'Is that a nautical term?'

'It is today.'

Reilly looked doubtful. 'I don't know. What about me? They're actively looking for me.'

'We keep you out of sight. I mean, they're pretty focused. But I'm confident in our abilities. Look...'

He pointed as the cop boat made a third pass, this time veering closer to the trawler to make it obvious they were interested. The gang ignored the police boat, sticking to what they were doing.

Bodie turned away. 'It's time to end this thing,' he said.

CHAPTER TWENTY SEVEN

Bodie gravitated towards Falmouth. He knew it served as a notable seaport and had a rich seafaring history. It was big and busy enough to offer the services he required. The team, still uncertain, made their way to the city and parked up near one of the docks.

'Who the hell's gonna sail the thing?' Cassidy asked. 'I have a lot of skills, but sailing ain't one of 'em.'

'Good question,' Bodie said, as if he hadn't thought that far ahead. 'I'm making this up as I go along.'

'I can tell.'

They looked around for a while and eventually found themselves in a small, dingy office facing a bespectacled woman who looked down at them over the top of her glasses. She was tall too, which gave the effect more gravitas. Bodie felt under inspection.

'You want to rent a boat?' she asked in a gravelly, cigarette-induced voice. 'For how long?'

Bodie went through the motions. It seemed that hiring a pilot wasn't all that difficult, too; there were plenty available. The woman's business seemed well set up for the task at hand.

And soon, they were standing on a dock, looking

up at their new boat. It was lacklustre at best, and had seen hard times. The pilot met them at the dock.

'I'm your helmsman,' he said. 'Is there an actual plan?'

Bodie studied him. The man carried a backpack and had a big black beard. His eyes sparkled blue through bushy eyebrows. His face was lined, craggy, his mouth a thin line that was currently curled up into a smile. He wore an old long coat and denim jeans. 'Name's Jeremy,' he said. 'But you can call me Captain.'

'Aye, aye,' Bodie said. 'Actually, we do have a plan.'

The team lugged their diving equipment aboard and were soon ready to set sail. But it was already late-afternoon. The captain came on deck and eyed them.

'Clouds rolling in.' He looked above. 'Forecast is bad all night. I suggest we start in the morning as tomorrow's going to be a very pretty day.'

Bodie checked the time. The day had got away from them and he hadn't realised. He didn't fancy starting the dive in the dark and decided the guy was right. They would begin first thing in the morning. The captain told them he'd stay the night aboard to look after supplies and bade them farewell. The team was left with nothing to do but head back to the hotel for another night of cold drinks and hot food and comfort, to prepare for what was to come. Bodie, at the bar later that night – just Cassidy and him left – leaned in to her and lifted his drink.

'Here's to what's to come,' he said.

'I hope you know what you're doing.'

'Always,' he said. 'Sometimes. Never. Yeah, that about covers it.'

'I wonder how long they've been out there.'

'Not long. My guess is a couple of days at the most. I'm hoping we have more experience.'

'We know where to look,' Cassidy said. 'We have a GPS fix, and all the right equipment. If the rock formation is there, we'll go straight to it. I just hope they didn't find it today.'

Bodie sobered slightly. 'My god, that's a foul thought to have at midnight. Be positive – they won't have. And even if they have, they won't be able to haul it all up. To be honest, when we find it, we'll have to contact the authorities, I think.'

'Then why the big ship?'

'Because we might *not* contact the authorities,' Bodie grinned, enjoying revealing his darker side. 'That suits me better.'

'They'll only squander it,' Cassidy smiled.

Bodie put a hand on hers. 'Thanks for sticking with me, Cass,' he said. 'I know it's a mad plan.'

'You're a bit drunk,' she said and then shrugged. 'I trust you. I'd go into hell for you.'

'And often have,' Bodie said, and then held his glass up. 'To what tomorrow brings,' he said.

'To going into hell.'

They parted and slept soundly. The entire team was up before the crack of dawn the next morning and were soon on their way back to the boat. This early, it was cold and misty outside, the whole environment echoing to the sound of chugging cars and lorries on the bypass outside. The day seemed diluted, as if they were the only part of it – everything else seeming surreal.

When they arrived at the docks it got worse. The mist was thicker, heavy tendrils curling around their faces. The only sounds were the lapping of waves at the dock and the creaking timbers of the nearby ships. It felt like a scene out of time, and Bodie got lost twice trying to find the ship. It was Lucie who eventually guided them the right way.

Eventually, they stood looking up at the stained and pitted off-white boat, taking deep breaths and imagining what they were going to be up against today. This could really be the calm before the storm.

Bodie led the way aboard and they were greeted cheerily by the Captain.

'You ready for a grand day at sea?' he asked them all.

There was a muted reply, none of them really looking forward to the prospect of diving. It had been decided that Bodie, Cassidy and Jemma – their most experienced divers – would go down to investigate the sea bed.

The captain showed them where he had already brewed coffee and then got about starting up the boat. He told them it should be a smooth day with little wind and little chop on the seas to worry about. The rising sun would soon burn off the fog and it would be a warm one. Bodie didn't think that would bother him being hundreds of feet under the waves.

Soon, the boat was leaving the harbour and heading out into the wider seas. Bodie and the others grouped together near the prow, staring pensively over the waters. Maybe they should slip into their diving gear, but Bodie didn't think it was warranted yet, as he was brooding about the first meeting with the Diablos.

Despite the police presence, how would they take it?

He didn't have to wait long to find out. The captain guided them skilfully out to sea and then followed Lucie's coordinates to the right place. As they approached, he stuck his head out of the cabin window.

'How close do you want me to get to that other boat?'

'Not too close,' Bodie said. 'We don't want to look like we're intimidating them.'

'No problem.'

The captain sailed them into a position just a few hundred feet from Lucie's GPS coordinates and then stopped, riding the waves. Bodie remained where he was, near the prow, with the others standing alongside him. They didn't stare at the other vessel, just watched the undulating seas all around and stared at the distant shore.

Reilly was down below, seated inside the boat with a grim expression on his face. He didn't necessarily agree with this plan of action, but hadn't come up with anything better.

Bodie watched the trawler out of the corner of his eyes. Both boats bobbed up and down in the still waters.

It took several minutes, but men started to come out and stare. Soon, Bodie saw three large guys leaning over the other boat's rails, dark expressions on their faces. He looked over at them and waved. They were too far away to start up any kind of conversation.

'Start moving about purposefully,' he said. 'Look like we're meant to be here.'

The team set about dragging out their diving gear and making it obvious that they were here for a reason. They wanted to see the other group's reactions as soon as possible. Bodie climbed into his suit on deck, grabbed a mask, his rebreather and a tank and let the others help him. He took his time, saving the flippers for last. To his right, Cassidy and Jemma were also climbing into their suits.

'Are they reacting?' Bodie asked at one point.

Heidi watched the other boat furtively. 'Oh, yeah, one of them went apeshit a while back. They appear to be having a meeting.'

'Interesting. I wonder what they'll do?'

As if on cue, the police boat made its first appearance of the day, making an obvious pass. Bodie half expected the vessel's occupants to stop alongside and maybe come up for a chat, but they didn't. The police passed on by without comment.

'That can't be good,' Heidi said suddenly.

Bodie moved with difficulty in the wetsuit. 'What's happening?'

'It looks like they're about to launch a boat. There's a lot of activity.'

'So that's what they're gonna do,' Bodie said. 'They see us suiting up, and they're heading over here.'

'It would seem so.'

Bodie turned to his fellow compatriots. 'Slow down,' he said. 'We're about to have company.'

CHAPTER TWENTY EIGHT

Three Diablos powered over to the boat and asked for permission to come aboard. They were large, powerful men, and there wasn't a smile between them. Bodie and the others greeted them with cheerful expressions and allowed them aboard without the hint of a complaint. Before the men actually boarded, Reilly was stowed away in a cupboard, much to his discontent, and told to wait there until the coast was clear.

Bodie led the newcomers below. There wasn't a lot of room, so it had to be Bodie, Heidi and Cassidy and the new guys. Time was already ticking on, and it was past mid morning by now.

Heidi offered them drinks, anything they wanted so long as it was coffee, water or beer. The men declined.

Bodie sat down and faced them. Still, they hadn't cracked a smile, but neither had they spoken. The first man was short and sat hunched, so that he appeared even shorter. He had a lined face and no eyebrows at all, which gave him a scary appearance. The second man was long and lanky and sat upright so that he appeared like a long-limbed giant. His eyes were as dark as the bottom of the ocean. The third man sat with his legs crossed and had an air of confidence. He regarded Bodie with an unruffled expression.

'What can we do for you, gentlemen?' Cassidy asked.

Bodie was quietly surprised at her tone. He'd never heard her sound so solicitous with potential enemies.

The laid back man leaned forward slightly and spoke with an American accent. 'We're here conducting a survey,' he said. 'Of the sea bed. Seabed mapping, collating, processing and validating data that we'll pass on to UKHO experts.'

The man left it at that. Short and sweet, more believable, Bodie assumed. He leaned forward and held his hand out. 'Good to meet you,' he said equably. 'My name is Bodie.'

The other man didn't smile, but shook hands. 'Palmer,' he said. The other two men didn't move a muscle, just sat there looking mildly threatening. Bodie ignored them.

'What are you going here?' Palmer asked.

'We're tourists,' Bodie said. 'Keen on diving. We keep a close eye on the local forums and people say this is a great spot for diving. Don't worry, we won't get in your way. You'll barely even notice us.'

Palmer couldn't stave off a grimace. 'Couldn't you dive somewhere else?'

'Are you kidding? Like I said we we're recommended this spot by people who are in the know. They say it's amazing.'

Palmer took a few moments to look around the interior, to study Cassidy and Heidi. His face remained stony.

'We'd really appreciate it if you vacated the general area.'

'Don't worry, we won't break anything.' Bodie met the man's hard eyes and didn't back down. He wondered how far the man would take the lie.

'It's our equipment,' Palmer said. 'It's very valuable. I wouldn't want to risk anything. Are you insured?'

Bodie almost laughed. It was a searching question if he was being honest. A good one. He decided to call the man's bluff. 'Yeah,' he said. 'We are.'

Palmer's lips tightened, and a flush of anger blossomed on his face. He appeared to be deciding what to do next. There was a heavy air of tension in the room, only deepened by the total silence of Heidi and Cassidy and the other two men. The atmosphere was becoming heavier by the minute.

'What are you really doing here?' Palmer finally said, breaking the pretence. 'You're not tourists.'

Bodie smiled confidently. 'And you're not here mapping the seabed either.'

'Why not?' Palmer's acting was actually quite good.

'What have you found so far?'

Bodie's question was blunt enough to make Palmer twitch. The man licked his lips, losing a little of his composure.

'We're not searching for anything,' he said. 'Are you?'

Bodie decided the falsehood had gone far enough. 'Oh, okay,' he said. 'We're here searching for the same thing you are. The Lady Royal. Can you handle a competitor?' He felt confident with the forceful admittance. The visitors were outnumbered and there was still the police boat to think about.

Palmer was silent for a while, trying to decide in which direction to jump. 'So you are here for the galleon?' he asked finally.

'The very one painted by Gustave Auch. We solved the clues, we followed the directions. All the way here.'

'We were here first.'

Bodie shrugged. 'It's a free world. The cops are close. We're peaceful people. Are you?'

Palmer scrunched his face up just as the other two men leaned forward. 'I'm warning you right now,' he said. 'Do not get in our way. There are no bounds to the hurt we will visit upon you.'

Bodie stayed quiet for a period, pretending that he was intimidated. 'We're just two competitive diving teams,' he said. 'Surely that's all just friendly rivalry.'

'We're not your friends, and we're not your rivals. You will leave the area or we will cause damage to you. Do I make myself clear?'

'We're not going anywhere,' Bodie said calmly. 'We intend to dive, and we intend to dive soon. But we will stay out of your way. If you provide us with a diagram of your intended movements, we'll avoid them.'

Palmer snarled at that. 'So you can see the areas we've already covered? Don't take me for an idiot. I'm giving you fair warning.'

Bodie didn't back down. 'And now I'm giving you warning. We have as much right to be here as you. We haven't taken it to the authorities either...but we could.'

Palmer looked astonished. 'Are you *threatening* me?'

'Not at all. Just pointing out one of the facts. We're both in this together.'

Now Palmer sat back, thinking hard. He was clearly wondering how far to take this today, deciding if he could get away with violence. Bodie's calm manner and the presence of the police boat would deter him, though. Even so, Bodie was ready for action.

Finally, Palmer sat forward, fists bunched. 'I'll give you one last warning,' he said. 'Back away. Back down. If you go ahead, we will cause you a lot of pain. I promise. The police don't bother us. We always find a way.'

'You're a long way from home,' Bodie said, revealing he knew more about them than they believed. 'Fishes out of water, so to speak. I don't believe you even know what you're doing. That's why you haven't found anything yet. I think you're inept, lacking, not in the same league as us. And if you want to fight, get on your goddamn feet.'

It was as in your face as he could get. He'd decided there was no more point beating around the bush. Intentions had been made clear. And now, all three visitors rose to their feet.

Bodie, Cassidy and Heidi rose too. The six figures faced each other with hard eyes and determined expressions. Bodie thought: *don't back down.*

'We'll see you on the seabed,' he whispered.

'You don't know what you're letting yourselves in for,' Palmer grated. 'We're not here to kill people.'

If it was gauged to terrorise, it didn't. Bodie showed not a single sign of fear. By now, he imagined, Palmer had figured out they were far more than simple tourists.

'May the best person win,' Cassidy spoke once more. 'Which will be us, obviously.'

The leader of the Diablos looked like he wanted to choke the life out of her right there and then. 'You should be careful who you insult.'

'Oh, if I was insulting you, you'd know about it, *boy*. Just take a walk.'

Bodie decided they had taken the confrontation about as far as it could go. He stepped aside so that Palmer and his cohorts could head for the door. 'After you,' he said.

Palmer glanced at his two goons, shook his head as if to ward off any action. He turned to the door and the bright day outside and started walking. With a hand on the door handle, he hesitated.

'You think you're better than us?' he said. 'You think you can walk away from this in one piece? It will not happen.'

Bodie stayed cool, not reacting. 'We'll see you in the water,' he said evenly.

Again, at the perfect time, he saw the police boat passing by outside on its constant loop. He made sure Palmer saw it. 'And I guess those guys will help keep the peace.'

He wasn't worried about the Diablos. He didn't think they had guns, and he didn't think they were any more than six-strong. Maybe they had a few hired divers too, but they weren't part of the crew. He didn't think they would act on anything until after they'd located the treasure.

Which, hopefully, would be a long time coming.

Smiling, he saw Palmer and his goons off the boat.

And then turned to Cassidy and Heidi, smiling.

'That was fun,' Cassidy said.

CHAPTER TWENTY NINE

Bodie, on the stroke of midday, approached the edge of the boat. He, Cassidy and Jemma were ready for their first dive. The vista was broad and glistening, open seas to all sides apart from the trawler. As he stood by the boat's rail, Bodie watched the activity on the other vessel.

Several men were standing at the rail, arms folded. They had clearly been told to watch the other vessel's activities and report. As Bodie stared back, he noticed two divers appear and prepare to jump overboard. Clearly, they were all going down together.

Lucie brought the GPS out and strapped it to his wrist. 'Just follow the dots,' she said with a smile.

Bodie nodded. He was slightly worried that, while he and the two women were down below, the Diablos might try something. But they had Yasmine, Heidi, Lucie and, if necessary, Reilly available up top, who were a formidable team. And there really was no option. He was going to have to go down.

He was sweating in the suit. The waves lapped at the side of the boat, making it roll under his flipper-shod feet. He took another look at the GPS and then back at Lucie. He gave her a thumbs-up.

Turned to Cassidy and Jemma. 'Are you both ready?'

'As I'll ever be,' Cassidy nodded at him.

Together, the trio launched themselves into the water.

Bodie descended through a thick murk almost immediately, the water pulling against him. He arrowed downwards, using his legs to power through the sea. Vaguely, on either side, he could make out the dull shapes of his companions.

It was a dark, black world of silence with little to stimulate the senses. Bodie hadn't been diving for years and hadn't really missed the experience. Now, he remembered the right things to do and made simple mistakes that he quickly rectified. It was all a new learning experience.

They descended hundreds of feet below the sea, dark figures plunging down. To their left, somewhere unknown, were their rivals, also following some kind of plan. Bodie did not know what it was, but was aware it hadn't really worked so far for them.

He sank until the seabed came upon him and then slowed. His feet touched the rocky bottom, all boulders and uneven ground and some kind of leafy life clutching to the jagged rocks. He crouched for a moment, waiting for his friends.

They also appeared on the GPS as two blue dots. They were close, and they were homing in on him using their own systems. Bodie crouched and waited, staring hard at his surroundings.

It was darkness and gloom, illuminated only by his suit's bright lights. Soon, he saw his friends cutting towards him through the dimness.

They regrouped on the seabed and tested their communications system.

'Can you hear me, okay?' Bodie asked.

There were two affirmations, and then the team studied the general area for a few minutes. Bodie then checked the GPS attached to his wrist.

'We head right,' he said, which was towards the Diablos boat unless he'd got entirely turned around. 'Let's try fifty yards.'

They swam in the right direction, now moving through their own silt that they'd kicked up from the bottom. A large fish swam close to Bodie, tracking him for a while, and then darted away.

Soon, they were stopping again and checking their positions. 'It should be just up ahead on the right,' Bodie said with some excitement in his voice.

They headed in the direction that put their blue dots over the treasure's green one. Bodie swam easily, not exerting himself too much and keeping it calm. The others were good divers and would follow a similar routine. They came to a large rock formation that made Bodie stop in his tracks.

'Hey,' he said. 'Is this it?'

Cassidy swam up and away from the giant rock, taking it in. 'Looks different,' she said. 'I can't tell.'

As Bodie swam around it, he saw another large rock just a few metres from the first. He narrowed his eyes underneath the face mask. 'Crap,' he said.

'What is it?' Jemma asked, also nonplussed by the rock.

'Looks like more than one,' Bodie said. 'A whole formation of them, I think.'

He could see several more outlines in the murk as he shined his light forwards. 'We're gonna have to pick between them.'

'How accurate is the GPS?' Cassidy asked.

'To a few feet, but it all falls apart right now. There are dozens of damn rock formations down here.'

'That must be what's slowing the Diablos down,' Jemma said.

Bodie checked his GPS. To be fair, the dots weren't exactly lined up yet. He told the others, and they started around the side of the large rock until they reached another, then swam to the left of that. They eased over the top of a third before Bodie saw the dots had come together. There, he stopped again.

'It should be right here,' he said.

They were floating about fifty feet above the bottom and looked down. Their lights illuminated several craggy rock formations, but no ship, no sunken galleon. Bodie glanced from left to right.

'Damn,' he said. 'This is gonna be harder than we thought.'

'We need some kind of mapping system,' Cassidy said.

'You think the Diablos will help?' Jemma asked in an ironic tone.

'I don't see any sign of them,' Bodie said, admittedly unable to see an awful lot in the murk. 'Maybe they don't have set coordinates like we do.'

'A lot of good they're doing us,' Cassidy worried.

They trod water for a while, and then Bodie checked his watch. 'Right,' he said. 'We still have quite a bit of time here. Let's do something useful.'

Working together, they searched among the rock formations, taking them one at a time. They swam down to the bottom and searched between stony hills, taking their time because, in the perpetual dark, it would be easy to miss something. Bodie darted left and right, going right to the bottom and then looking up and up, over the top and back down on the other side. Finding any part of the wreckage would help pinpoint it.

An hour passed. Their excitement faded. Bodie felt more and more that their search was becoming fruitless and they needed more structure to it. They were wasting time down here when they could be up top, mapping out some kind of search grid. He combed formation after formation, finding nothing but the flora and fauna of the sea.

Eventually, he pulled the other two together. They all stood in the valley created by two large crags.

'This isn't gonna work,' he said. 'We need to head back up top and work it out. We're wasting our time down here.'

'Agreed,' Cassidy said. 'There are simply too many rocks to pinpoint the exact one.'

Jemma also capitulated, and soon, the team were heading back up through the waters. Above, the day was still bright and provided some illumination to head for.

Bodie's head broke the surface of the sea close to the boat. The first thing he did was to call Lucie.

'We need another plan,' he yelled. He tried to hang on to the thought that it hadn't been an entirely unproductive day. At least they'd investigated the general area and knew what to expect. But tomorrow would be a far better day.

CHAPTER THIRTY

Lucie spent a long afternoon using online data to map the seabed.

Bodie and the others supported her by being close, eating and drinking, and enjoying a few laughs. Lucie was the only one with the skills to do what she was doing and made sure she got it right. There could be no mistakes this time.

To their right, the Diablo's vessel swayed in the calm sea, looking serene and unruffled. There was little activity on board, something Bodie took as a good sign.

The captain stayed at the helm, happy with his own company. Bodie and the others sat around the inner cabin with a rough wooden table in the centre. They had glasses full of wine and spirits and mixers and a goodly portion of food. The food, being aboard the boat, was relatively poor fayre, but it would do them for one night. Funnily enough, Bodie thought, as he looked at the table, the plates of fruit were the only things left untouched.

Lucie tapped away on her laptop in a tight corner of the room, legs drawn up, totally engrossed in her work.

Bodie had decided, since there was nothing else they could do tonight, that they might as well let loose. He trusted the captain to look after the boat and thought a night at sea enjoying a party atmosphere might be just what they all needed. He also thought it would help make the Diablos lessen their guard a little if they heard the merriment coming from the other boat.

So, Bodie poured the drinks and dolled out the food and started several conversations. Soon, the entire team apart from Lucie was involved.

'What happens when we find the treasure?' Reilly said, drink to his lips.

'I like your confidence,' Cassidy said. 'In case you didn't know, that's what the boat's for.'

Bodie shook his head, acknowledging Cassidy's joke. 'It'll need pinpointing and then the government's will get involved, I guess. We may have to bring some of it up.'

'Lifting equipment?' Reilly asked.

'Maybe. But by that time the find is ours. The relic hunters will be back.' He saluted them all with his drink.

Lucie, from her place in the corner, shook her head. 'The relic hunters went nowhere,' she said. 'They've just been biding their time, waiting for another mission.'

'And this one just fell in our laps,' Cassidy said. 'Like a fucking alligator.'

Bodie laughed. 'Yeh, it certainly has teeth,' he said. 'But, so far, the police presence is keeping the Diablos at bay.'

'You don't think they'll try anything?' Heidi asked.

'Have you seen their boat? They already have the heavy lifting equipment on board. They're hoping to steal this treasure, fly completely under the radar.'

'In front of the cops?'

Bodie shrugged. 'They'll have a plan. Maybe they're global and powerful enough to hand out a bribe. Maybe they know someone in charge. I think *they're* just biding their time, waiting until they find the treasure.'

'It won't happen,' Yasmine said. 'Not while we're around.'

'Agreed,' Bodie reached out to top her wine glass up. 'Who'd have thought that when we started helping Reilly avoid his old gang we'd end up here in the English Channel searching for a lost galleon and a load of treasure?'

'All thanks to Gustave Auch,' Lucie said.

Bodie proposed another salutation, this one to the master painter. Outside, night now pressed hard against the windows and a fresh, light squall blew in. It speckled the windows with raindrops and set the waves in motion so that the boat rocked slightly. It wasn't uncomfortable, just something to be a little wary of.

'I may sleep right here,' Bodie said.

'I think you're gonna have to,' Cassidy said. 'This boat only has two beds.'

'I thought we might all bunk in together.'

'You and Heidi want company, do you?'

Bodie laughed.

'What's wrong? The frizz bomb not enough for you, Guy?'

Heidi gave Cassidy a weary look. 'You still calling me that? I thought that was because you didn't like me.'

'It's what you'll always be to me.'

Bodie sought to change the subject. 'Anyone think the Diablos have mapped the bottom too? They're clearly aware of mapping.'

'It could be what's taking them so long,' Lucie said. 'There's a lot to map, as I'm finding out. The rock formations are a solid square half mile from end to end and there's a lot of them.'

'That still gives them a day or two head start on us,' Cassidy said.

'Doesn't matter,' Bodie replied. 'We might get lucky the moment our feet touch the bottom.'

The conversation turned and turned. The drinks flowed, and the food was consumed slowly. Bodie's team sat side by side and enjoyed each other's company, the camaraderie, the togetherness. The light rain stroked the windows and a steady breeze rocked the boat and they never felt any of it. They were happy in each other's company, engrossed in the night.

Bodie knew all too well that it was the calm before the storm.

CHAPTER THIRTY ONE

Early the next morning, Bodie, Cassidy and Jemma were again standing by the ship's rail, waiting to climb down the ladder into the sea. Bodie felt a little thick-headed, but didn't think it was anything that would impede him.

This time, their GPS systems showed a security grid with dotted lines they could follow. As they walked, the dotted lines would become solid, showing where they had walked. Lucie had programmed enough dotted lines to last them several hours.

Bodie waited for the signal. Across the waves, he noted the Diablos boat was quiet – its occupants still apparently sleeping or breakfasting. He nodded at Cassidy and Jemma and then held up a hand.

'Let's do this.'

The trio climbed down into the waves, went under, and started on their way down. Blackness soon enveloped them. Soon, they hit the bottom and Bodie started to follow his map, finding the beginning and then following the dotted line as best he could. Lucie had programmed them to lead around the rock formations, but it wasn't entirely accurate. The going was hard, leading them over rocky crags and pitfalls, but they were able to swim over the worst of it.

Bodie soon lost track of time. He put his head down and sought to complete the circuit at a decent pace, not going too fast or too slow.

He saw shoals of fish darting and dashing this way and that. At one point, an entire shoal enveloped him, tiny objects filling his visor like a mini, glistening whirlwind. He stood calmly for half a minute until they passed by, teeth gritted, listening as Cassidy laughed. At one point, he saw an underwater arch and made a detour towards it, reminded of their findings in Atlantis. Maybe he hoped for the vestiges of a hidden city, the beginning of another relic hunt, but all he found was another anomaly, just a natural arch in the rock.

Cassidy and Jemma followed, and then, one by one, took the lead. They all led the way at some point, taking the pressure off the others. It was a sensible routine that kept up the pace.

Hours passed. Bodie was reaching the end of the dotted line map. He was currently in front and saw that there was only a short way left to go, which he calculated at about fifteen minutes. It had been a long, hard slog, if he was being honest, and he wasn't looking forward to having to do it again. But Lucie had told them she had at least three days' worth of maps, and that they all had to be followed.

He was currently in a dip on the seabed, a field of waving plantlife to his left, a pile of rock to his right. Ahead, a spectacular rock formation rose out of the gloom, something with a sharp peak and angled sides. Immediately, he thought it looked familiar.

It looked exactly like the rock in the painting.

Bodie slowed. He turned quickly to Cassidy and Jemma.

'Ahead,' he said. 'That's the very rock that Gustave Auch painted.'

Cassidy and Jemma craned their necks as best they could. 'Looks like it,' Cassidy said.

Bodie, sure of his findings, moved forward slowly. Ahead, the seabed dipped, forming a deeper hole which he had to swim across. When his feet touched the other side, he was right up against the rock.

To the right, he spied an anomaly.

Bodie knew the sight wasn't correct. He'd spent enough time on this godforsaken seabed to know by now that what he saw shouldn't be there. It was spikey in places, rounded in others, and it wasn't made of rock.

'Follow me,' he said, voice high.

They filed around the great rock, following a path in its base that curved at a gentle rate. The rock towered over them. Bodie, walking too fast now, stirred up a load of silt, and had to slow down as the clouds obscured his vision. After a while, he was ready to move again and steadily approached the irregularity.

Getting close, he stopped, his lights illuminating the darkness. Their combined beams fell upon a wooden object – the side of a ship.

There was a shipwreck right here at the bottom of the sea!

Bodie advanced. He could see a curved hull and lots of wooden planking. The ship appeared to be on its side and several of its beams had broken apart, probably shattering on impact. Bodie swam up to it and laid his hand on the wood, stroking the side if only to prove to himself that it was real. That it was, in fact, tangible.

He couldn't get any closer, he thought with a smile. He wished there was a way to tell Lucie what he had found, but their communications system wasn't sophisticated enough to reach the surface. It was simply three-way between them. Now, he used it.

'We have to find out if it's the right ship first,' he said. 'We have to locate the name.'

'Do you remember where it was situated?' Cassidy asked.

Bodie nodded before remembering they couldn't really see the gesture. 'Yeah,' he said. 'I do.'

He kicked off, swimming up the wooden side of the ship. The shape of it revealed further that he was heading for the prow, which was exactly where he wanted to be. His lights showed him the way.

Soon, he was in the right position to check the name of the ship.

It appeared out of the gloom, old and weary and worn by its time under the sea. But there was no doubt about the lettering.

Lady Royal.

They'd found it. Found the very ship they were looking for, something that had rested here for hundreds of years just waiting to be discovered. Bodie felt a thrill and a shiver pass through the length of his body.

'We found it,' he said.

Jemma let out a victory whoop. Cassidy was more reserved, swimming up to Bodie's position and taking a look for herself.

'Now that's a thing of beauty,' she said.

Bodie pinpointed the exact position on the GPRS as he savoured the moment. Even close up to the ship, it was hard to make out the full bulk of it, and he knew they'd probably have to get specialist equipment in to lift out the heavier items. But there was no harm in taking a look first.

'Hey,' he said to the others. 'Wanna get a look inside?'

Cassidy was always up for anything. 'Let's go.'

Jemma was more conservative. 'We've already been down here a while,' she said. 'Maybe we should come back later now we know exactly where it is.'

They trod water, Bodie and Cassidy hyped up for the search, but not wanting to gainsay Jemma. Around them, underwater shadows moved in creepy tandem, urged by the flow of water. Bodie stared hard when one of those shadows broke away and started moving with a purpose.

Straight towards them.

CHAPTER THIRTY TWO

Bodie stared in shock and disbelief.

'What the hell...?'

Through the gloom, three swimmers were cutting towards them. Dark shapes, dark motives – the figures were moving purposefully.

'We have company,' Bodie pointed. Jemma and Cassidy turned to look. The waters felt calm all around them, but the situation was anything but composed.

'Shit, it's the Diablos,' Cassidy said. 'They found it too.'

Bodie had already come to the same conclusion. He moved to intercept the approaching divers, holding up a hand. Of course, they couldn't communicate down here, but he could at least try to ward them off.

The divers floated just a few feet away, three on each side, facing each other.

Bodie held up a hand, pointed to himself and then waved the three divers away. To him, the communication was clear. *We found it; you didn't. Now leave it alone.*

A man swam forward, identifying himself as the leader. He shook his head rapidly and then held up a fist. Bodie stared at it. What the hell...?

It was a signal. All the divers pounced forward. The lead diver engaged Bodie, throwing a fist at his head. Bodie saw it coming easily and, even though feeling nonplussed and surreal, dodged out if the way.

Are you kidding me?

These guys really wanted to start a fight down here. Bodie guessed they wanted to reveal their dominance at the earliest possible stage. Maybe they had direct communication with the ship and had received orders. Either way, as he fought, he couldn't believe what was happening.

His adversary threw one punch and then another, both aimed for Bodie's face. They travelled through the water slowly, easily avoidable, but then Bodie moved more slowly too. He skipped back, out of range for a moment, and held up a hand.

Don't do this.

But the man didn't listen. His comrades were engaging Cassidy and Jemma, swimming headlong against them. Bodie saw punches and kicks being delivered.

He had more than enough to contend with. His opponent came in with a kick to the stomach that Bodie found hard to evade. It landed squarely and was more of a push back than a kick. Yet Bodie was moved hard in the water and felt the blow. He struggled to maintain his balance. The man came at him again, throwing more punches. Bodie still couldn't get his head around it, but he thought this guy might actually have some experience fighting under water.

The two men struggled. Bodie started to realise his adversary was trying to get close and thought he knew why. The guy would try to remove his mask and his air valve. This man was actually trying to kill him.

Still reeling, Bodie fought to stay out of the man's way. They drifted away from the Lady Rose and ended up fighting on the bottom of the sea, undulating under the dark waters. Bodie tripped on a rock, then almost went headlong when his foot was hooked by a swaying plant.

The man pushed his advantage, finally getting up close to Bodie. He struck Bodie's ribs; the blows telling. As Bodie folded, the man reached out for his face mask.

Bodie felt the other man's gloves on his face, felt the fingers curl around his mask. He jerked back violently. The other man forced his way closer.

Cassidy swam out of range of her attacker, giving him space. She saw his movements, the range of his attack. It wasn't impressive. She waited for him to strike, and then just struck back, punishing the only vulnerable areas she could see – his neck, his ribs, his groin. Already, she could tell, his heart wasn't fully in the fight.

The man came at her half-heartedly. She skipped to one side, span, and clubbed him over the back of the head. Out of the corner of her eye she could see Bodie struggling with his own opponent and swam closer just in case she was needed. Her opponent didn't notice the manoeuvre and just lunged at her once again.

Jemma swam in and out, taunting her opponent with her speed. The guy was big and slow, and couldn't seem to couldn't seem to compensate for her lightness and speed. Out of the water he would have been a handful, but down here...she was more than his equal. The man lumbered at her. Jemma had time to gauge his attack, to figure out where he was aiming, to think of a response and then execute it. All before his blow landed. The only trouble was – she wasn't punishing him enough.

Bodie retaliated by reaching out for his opponent's mask, figuring a like for like attack was the only recourse. The two men stood toe to toe and grappled and fumbled and drifted around the rocks. Bodie saw an opening, raised both legs and then planted them hard in the other guy's stomach. The two men flew away from each other, the weight of the water pulling them down.

The other guy struggled, clearly in pain. Bodie had hit him cleanly and with force. The trouble was, he thought, this fight was going nowhere. They had already pinpointed the Lady Rose and now they had to get the hell away, back to the boat. This confrontation was useless to them.

Bodie's opponent tried to shrug off the pain. Bodie gave him no respite. He swam in and launched a couple of punches, both to the man's head. Maybe he would get lucky and break the mask. Maybe he'd dislodge it. The other guy jerked out of the way, his movements slow but beneficial. He evaded Bodie's attack.

The man swam back, arms out, feet kicking. Bodie chased him through the churned up waters, striking out. He had the advantage now and didn't want to lose it. The man kept swimming back, so fast he collided with the side of the Lady Rose.

Brought a hand up to his head and lurched.

Bodie saw a trail of blood in the water. The man

had cut himself, and saw it too. He whirled, the stream of blood flowing behind him. Bodie didn't let him off the hook, though. This guy was trying to kill him. He swam right up to the man and started swinging.

The guy kicked out, slamming a foot into Bodie's ribs. He flew back; the pain stabbing through him. Even now, they were clearly equally matched. Bodie saw the man back away, saw him look for his companions. Bodie took a quick look, too.

Cassidy was darting around her opponent and landing blow after blow. The guy already looked defeated, though Bodie noticed she hadn't fully ended the fight by ripping off his mask or damaging his air valves. She hadn't taken a hit, and looked as fresh as if she was taking a stroll in the park.

Jemma struggled with her large opponent, but was staying easily out of his reach at the same time as being incapable of hurting him. Still, she tried, tearing in at every opportunity.

Bodie saw the fight go out of his opponent. Now was the time to press the issue, but did he really want to? Did he want a dark, unnatural, silent fight to the death hundreds of feet below the churning waves in the middle of this godforsaken area?

He relented, stopped going after his opponent. The man noticed immediately and held a hand up. At the same time, he must have spoken to his companions, because they also disengaged, swimming away from Jemma and Cassidy.

Bodie watched as the three men came together, spoke for a minute and then started powering away. The leader left a blood trail in his wake as Bodie watched them disappear into the murk.

Jemma and Cassidy swam up to him.

'Are you both okay?' he asked.

'Yeah, I can barely believe that happened,' Jemma said.

'It was quite fun,' Cassidy said, grinning under her mask. 'Something different.'

'For you maybe,' Bodie said. 'My guy had done that before.'

'I noticed you were under pressure. Don't worry, if you'd looked like you were in trouble, I'd have come to help.'

'Thanks.'

Jemma turned her attention to the wrecked galleon. 'So now what do we do about this? They too know exactly where it is.'

'Bad luck,' Bodie said. 'Just bad luck. But then, I guess they have been at this for days.'

'We're gonna have to get back up top fast,' Cassidy said, looking up. 'We don't want to give them too much of a head start on us.'

Bodie nodded in the gloom. He patted the side of the ship. 'See you soon, friend,' he said. 'I hope you have something good for us.'

Together, they started up towards the surface.

CHAPTER THIRTY THREE

Bodie broke the surface at speed, knowing it was essential that, now they had found the sunken ship, everything happened fast. To his right, Jemma and Cassidy appeared at the same time, their heads streaming with displaced water.

Bodie swam to the side of the ship and grabbed hold of the ladder. Soon, he was scurrying up the side, looking out for the others. He couldn't help but glance towards the other boat – the Diablos' trawler.

For now, the decks were quiet. Maybe the divers were explaining their find.

Bodie knew he had to do the same. There was no telling what the Diablos would do. He looked a little desperately for the police boat, but it was nowhere in sight. They never were when you really needed them, he thought, but plan something even a bit dodgy and they were all over you.

He shrugged it off, climbed aboard the boat, and looked for his onboard companions. Jemma and Cassidy were right behind him, already taking off their gear.

Bodie ran into the main cabin, struggling to get his air tanks off his back. The others stood around, taking a break. They looked surprised to see him, their eyes widening. On the contrary, Heidi smelled immediate trouble – her own eyes narrowing.

'What's wrong?'

'A few things,' Bodie said, fighting to get out of his gear. 'First, we found the Lady Royal. We found the ship.'

Lucie surged to her feet, ecstatic. 'That's bloody amazing,' she said. 'Great work, you three.'

Bodie nodded. 'Thanks.'

'But that's not all?' Heidi pressed.

Bodie shook his head. 'We were surprised down there. Three Diablo divers appeared and tried to kill us. They got away and are now aboard the other ship. God knows what's happening.'

Reilly went over to the window. 'Looks pretty quiet at the moment.'

'At the moment,' Bodie echoed. 'But they've already played their hand. I don't think they'll hesitate to go further. And now they also know where the Lady Royal is.'

'That is bad news,' Heidi admitted as Yasmine joined Reilly at the window. 'I wish we were armed.'

'Well, I don't think they are,' Bodie said. 'So it'll be an even contest.'

'Don't talk about contests,' Cassidy shuddered. 'Not after our last mission.'

Bodie changed quickly in the room and then joined the others at the window. 'What's the next step?' Lucie asked them.

Bodie turned to her. 'Under the circumstances, I think we should go straight to the authorities. If we were alone, I'd say yeah, let's do a bit of searching, but the presence of the Diablo boat changes everything.'

'No relic hunting?' Lucie asked with a pout.

'Sorry, but the circumstances have changed.'

'And they're about to change again,' Cassidy said as she peered through the window. 'Look.'

Bodie turned swiftly. The deck of the other boat was suddenly swarming with men. Within seconds, the boat turned around and started to point towards them. Bodie stared at it with mounting concern.

'Are they coming over here?' he asked, not entirely surprised but hopeful he was wrong.

'I think so,' Yasmine said. 'They'll be spoiling for a fight.'

'If it's anything like we just witnessed,' Jemma said. 'It'll be a fight to the death. Do we run?'

'We don't have time,' Bodie said. 'Look.'

The Diablo's boat was already flying through the waters, bouncing as it closed the gap between them. Bodie looked up as the captain put his head around the corner. 'Looks like we have some company coming,' he told them.

'Lock yourself in the helm,' Bodie told him. 'Stay out of this. It could get messy.'

The captain's face went white, and he quickly disappeared. Bodie watched as the Diablo's boat closed in still further. The gap reduced until the other boat was floating alongside, just far enough away so as not to crash.

He ran out to the side of the boat, facing the other. The deck was lined with men, all hard, craggy faces and severe expressions. Now they looked like the gang they really were, and they looked ready to do harm.

'What do you want?' Cassidy yelled.

Bodie gauged just how far away they were as the two boats bobbed alongside each other in the calm waters. The sun was high and bright, illuminating the entire scene. He looked for the leader of the Diablos, saw a man step forward.

Palmer.

'You found the ship,' the man said calmly.

'As did you.'

Palmer spread his arms. 'That's your loss. And how the hell did you expect to raise the treasure out of the water without alerting us?'

'Didn't think that far ahead. We're happy to hand this all over to the authorities.'

Palmer's face twisted. 'Well, we're not,' he said. 'And I'm pretty sure you know that already. Jesus Christ – is that Reilly?'

Bodie's face fell. He turned to see Reilly staring through a nearby window, trying to listen in. It really was all going from bad to worse.

Palmer turned back to Bodie. 'Give it up,' he said. 'Walk away now and we'll let you live.'

Bodie stared at him. 'Are you serious?' he didn't think Palmer's words matched what he knew of the Diablo's reputation.

'Not really.'

Palmer gesticulated, and there was a stentorian cry from his men all along the deck. The men fell back and then started running and then launched themselves across the gap between the boats, landing on the deck close to Bodie and the others. They then staggered and went head first, some losing their balance. But others stood their ground and were suddenly in the faces of the relic hunters.

Bodie was reminded of pirates of old swinging between ships, but then he had no more time to think as he came face to face with a jumping opponent. Still, the men were leaping across the two decks, landing hard on his own, flying through the air with yells and screams. The relic hunters all backed away in shock.

Palmer made the jump too, climbing onto his own rail and then jumping across the small gap. He landed on two feet and immediately challenged Reilly through the window.

'Come out and fight me!'

Bodie realised he had a close-up fight on his hands. A man was near him, muscles straining and an uncompromising look on his face. He swung at Bodie with a clenched fist, knocked him back two steps and then, from his waist, drew a knife.

He smirked.

Bodie fixed his gaze on the new threat. So these assholes were armed, it seemed. The knife thrust at him. Bodie let it fly harmlessly past, caught it between his arm and his ribs and then twisted. The knife pulled away from its owner and clattered to the deck. The man suddenly looked shocked and a bit cowed.

Bodie punched him in the face, saw blood fly from a broken nose. It was crowded all along the deck. His own team was battling several other foes, all of them taking up the available space. It was a melee, a chaotic clash of bodies.

Bodie drove a fist into his opponent's stomach, doubling him over, then sent a knee to the man's face. The guy collapsed to his knees. Bodie looked over the top of his body, saw another man take his place. His team was outnumbered, but the lack of space was mostly hindering the Diablos. Bodie saw flashes of sharp steel everywhere and knew the other team had brought a load of knives to a fistfight.

Palmer had dragged Reilly out into the open. He assailed the man now, his face evilly twisted.

'Where've you been, bastard?' he yelled. 'We've been scouring the world for you. You should know you'll never escape the reach of the Diablos.'

Reilly fought back hard, showing his skills. He didn't speak, just blocked and ducked and retaliated. He sought only to break bones and debilitate, let his punches and kicks do the talking. Palmer soon shut up, forced to fight properly.

Bodie fell against the rail. By now, all the Diablos had crossed. Their own boat was empty save for the captain and, maybe, a few neutral divers. Bodie had one man in his face and another to the right. He blocked and struck out, wary of knives.

All around him, the battle raged.

CHAPTER THIRTY FOUR

Cassidy ducked, grabbed her opponent around the middle and lifted. She figured one less Diablo aboard the boat wouldn't hurt. The man quickly realised her intent and grabbed hold of the rail as she lifted him past it in a grip of iron. Cassidy stumbled. His grip was too strong. She contented herself with several strikes to the ribs as he clung on, defenceless.

Heidi and Jemma were stuck near the prow, trying to find some extra room. The side of the boat was packed with fighters. Heidi backpedalled a few feet, taking two fighters with her. Jemma was at her side.

Together, the two women hit out, making the men block. One of them reached for a knife, but Heidi kicked his wrist just as he pulled it out. The weapon twanged and flickered in the light and then flew away high over the rail, spinning as it went. The man looked after it as if missing an old friend.

Heidi sprang at him, taking advantage.

Bodie could see Yasmine helping to shield Lucie from the worst of it. The historian was sheltering behind the woman, but striking out where and when she could, showing confidence. Bodie fought to get closer to them, knowing Yasmine couldn't completely safeguard Lucie on her own.

A man landed close to him, having only just jumped over the rail. He was unbalanced. Bodie took full advantage of that, raising a foot and planting it firmly in the man's solar plexus. His kick sent the man crashing against the rail, unbalancing, almost toppling overboard. Bodie saw his chance and didn't let up. He ran and shoulder barged the man in the chest. His momentum sent the man flying over the rail and falling between the two boats, smashing into the water and thrashing his arms about.

Bodie turned quickly, straight into another attack. This man had both hands raised and was bringing them down hard on Bodie's head. He couldn't dodge the attack. He felt it hit hard, saw dark spots, and staggered. Almost at once, he felt a blow to the ribs. He went down to one knee.

Bodie knew there was no help close by. He had to recover. At ground level, he knew there was only one hope. He reached out, grabbed the man's legs, and pulled. The man collapsed, landing on the deck spine first. All the air went out of him and he grunted loudly.

Bodie took a few seconds to recover. There were legs to left and right, most of them belonging to Diablos. He saw the man he'd flattened starting to rise.

Bodie didn't jump up. He swivelled and kicked out, catching the man with a solid blow in the mouth. The man's head flew back, blood coating his teeth as his lips mashed. He now collapsed completely to the deck, lying flat out.

Bodie struggled to his feet, head still ringing. The relic hunters were caught spread out along the side of the boat, cut off from each other. They were all engaging opponents, but since the Diablos had a few more and were competent fighters, this was only going to go one way.

Bodie had to help thin the herd.

He smashed his way past another man, moved in on one who was facing the other way. Using surprise, Bodie elbowed him in the neck and then threw him towards the rail. When the man hit Bodie was already in the air, leading with a front kick. His blow unbalanced the man and flipped him over the rail to the sea below.

Two down. No time to rest. Bodie moved on to the next man.

Reilly fought Palmer, the two men evenly matched. Reilly staggered into a side table, grabbed a lamp, and threw it at the other man. Palmer ducked and swatted it aside, kept coming.

'Where did you go?' the leader of the Diablos asked, gritting his teeth. 'Did you crawl into some rat hole and sit there for years?'

'It doesn't matter,' Reilly said, covering up as Palmer unleashed several blows. 'So long as it was away from you people.'

'You people?' Palmer echoed. 'We trusted you, believed in you. Helped you. Made you a part of our world. You betrayed us.'

'*Betrayed* you? You're a fucking criminal gang. A bunch of psychos. You murder for money, for land, for honour. I bettered myself. The only way I could get away from all that was to run.'

'We are the Diablos,' Palmer said. 'And our name means something.' He kicked out savagely, almost breaking Reilly's kneecap.

Reilly danced back, running out of room in the cramped cabin. The backs of his legs were up against a chair. He stopped, made ready for Palmer's next assault.

It came quickly. The man saw that Reilly was against the chair and gave him no respite. He charged forward, punching as he came. Reilly had to take the blows, covering up as best he could but flinching every time Palmer landed one. He tried to inch away, to the side, anywhere, but there just wasn't enough room.

Palmer threw punches right and left, trying to wear Reilly down. Reilly scurried onto the table at his back, kneeling, not knowing what else to do but determined to get out of the line of fire.

Palmer faced the man kneeling on the table. 'You will regret running away.'

Reilly used the time to bring his legs forward and smash Palmer in the chest with a two-footed kick. Palmer staggered away, affording Reilly some room. Now, he jumped at Palmer, coming down from a height with a tremendous blow that crashed down onto the other man's skull. Palmer staggered away, grunting.

Cassidy managed to join Jemma and Heidi at the boat's prow. Together, the three of them were a much more formidable team, fighting for each other. Together. They formed a triangle and held the Diablos off with ease.

But holding their enemy off wasn't moving forward. Bodie could see the three women at the front of the boat and saw that they'd downed two Diablos. Together with the two he'd thrown overboard, that probably just about matched both opposing forces up. But the relic hunters had already taken quite a bit of damage.

Bodie was bruised and cut and scraped. His ribs hurt. His thigh throbbed from where someone had viciously kicked it. He could see Yasmine staggering with every step. He couldn't see Reilly, but knew he'd have his hands full with Palmer. Even Lucie was bleeding from the head.

A terrifying thought occurred to him.

We're never going to beat the Diablos like this.

Even as he watched, Cassidy took a massive blow to the head. Yasmine was cut on the wrist. Lucie fell to her knees. Jemma barely avoided the chop of a serrated blade. The Diablos were systematically wearing them down.

Bodie made a fast decision. He disengaged from the battle and pushed his way to the back of the boat. Out of it for a few moments, he fished his phone out of his pocket.

Made the call.

Bodie contacted the emergency services, gave them a quick rundown of what was happening and where they were. He hoped the police boat would be local, maybe something even bigger. But he knew they really needed help.

With the call made, he jumped back into the fray.

CHAPTER THIRTY FIVE

The relic hunters finally managed to join up near the prow of their boat. They were seven strong, Reilly having climbed out through a window to join them once he noticed them teaming up. As they stood together, as they lined up, there was a brief lull in the battle. Bodie's chest heaved. They were all spent.

The Diablos bunched up before them. They, too, were damaged and breathing heavily. None of them were without pain. Around the deck, several of their colleagues lay, either unconscious or too injured to take part in the battle. Clouds had scudded in overhead now and there was the sting of sleet in the air. The sea all around them remained calm, almost mirror-like, as both boats bobbed together, just a few feet apart.

Bodie saw Palmer emerge from the same window as Reilly. The leader of the Diablos appeared to be surprised to see them all standing. He glanced at his men.

'I'm disappointed,' he said.

Everyone was trying to get their breath back. No one answered Palmer. Also, nobody pointed out that he'd had only one opponent the entire time and hadn't managed to negate him either.

Bodie then stepped carefully stepped forward. 'You have a chance,' he said. 'A chance to escape. The police are on their way. Escape is your only option, but you have to do it now.'

Palmer laughed and looked at the surrounding seas. 'Police? Are they invisible?'

'They're coming, believe me.'

'Even if they are, we will take care of them. The police do not scare the Diablos.'

Bodie wasn't quite sure how to answer that. He felt the strength returning to his limbs, felt his heart rate decline a little. Within the crowd of Diablos facing him, he saw the flash of three knives.

'You're really going to try to kill us?'

'Kill you and take your ship.'

'It's a boat,' Cassidy said sarcastically.

Palmer ignored her and turned to his men. 'Take them,' he said. 'And do it properly this time.'

The Diablos attacked. Bodie stood at the front of his team, ready to take the onslaught. A man flew at him with gusto, knife raised, and brought it down hard. Bodie blocked the attack with a raised wrist, the knife inches from his throat. He grabbed the wrist, twisted it, but the man twisted in the same direction, saving a broken bone. The problem for him then was that he was now standing side on to Bodie.

Which left him open to a rising knee that broke two ribs. The man squealed and slumped, half falling to the deck. Bodie helped him on his way with a kick to the side of the neck.

Cassidy was at his side, a solid wall of muscle. She blocked one attacker with a raised elbow that smashed his nose and got in the way of another man so that he ran straight into her and bounced off. He hit the deck at her feet, stunned. She kicked him full in the face.

Bodie saw light at the end of the tunnel. Working together like this, they were making headway against their enemies. The prow of the boat was crowded and getting slick with rain.

Just then, something caught his eye. There was a shape on the water a few miles away and it was getting closer.

A good size coastguard ship.

Bodie recognised it. He whirled to Palmer to point it out.

'They're coming.'

Palmer, engaged with Yasmine this time, pulled away to stare, but didn't issue any more orders to his men. Instead, he stepped back into the fight.

Bodie threw punches as more men confronted him. His knuckles ached, but he knew he couldn't let up, not even for a second. A knife flashed then, slicing his jacket at the right bicep. Luckily, the blade didn't cut skin. Bodie pulled away from the next strike, defending carefully.

The coastguard ship came closer and closer. It was about the same size as the trawler and Bodie's boat, but appeared to have figures crowded on to the deck. The trouble was, Bodie thought, those approaching figures wouldn't be able to tell the good guys from the bad guys.

What would happen when they arrived?

The ship narrowed the gap. Bodie downed another man, who crawled off through a forest of legs. By now, he could make out faces on the oncoming deck and saw how carefully the ship was approaching. A man with a radio was standing prominently on deck, looking as if he meant business.

'Stand down!' a voice suddenly rang out. 'All aboard the boat...stand down.'

Bodie would have loved to, but the Diablos weren't listening. The battle raged. Punches were thrown and deflected, bodies were pitched into action without concern. Palmer struggled to get the better of Yasmine, but he was wearing her down. All the relic hunters were being worn down as multiple attacks came at them.

The coastguard ship drifted close, now coming around to the other side of Bodie's boat. Soon, the vessel was alongside. The captain again tried to achieve a semblance of order.

'Stop what you are doing and stand down immediately!'

The Diablos ignored the command. Bodie and his team tried to step away, showing they were willing to disengage, but the Diablos came on, chasing their prey.

Bodie had to defend himself. He fended off an attack by a tall bald man and then spun away. He turned to the coastguard vessel and the men aboard.

'Help us!'

The ship's crew sprang into action. They wouldn't just leap across decks as the Diablos had, but they did possess a contraption that allowed them to cross between floating vessels. They started crossing steadily, a man at a time, and soon added to the number aboard Bodie's boat. The men from the coastguard wore white shirts and black jackets and were easily identifiable.

Soon, they were approaching the battle. Bodie took a blow to the head, staggered back, whirled to one of the men.

'They have weapons,' he said. 'And they're dangerous criminals. Be careful.'

The man turned and yelled out a warning to his colleagues. Bodie then saw something that made him smile. The men from the coastguard were armed. As one, almost, they withdrew their weapons and trained them on the Diablos.

The relic hunters sought to pull apart. The Diablos were momentarily isolated with the coastguard training their weapons upon them.

'Don't move,' someone cried.

Palmer stopped, staring at the newcomers who were climbing aboard Bodie's boat. He counted eight of them, crowding the far side and trying to come up onto the prow. It was a busy area, and only a couple of them could make it at a time. For a moment, there was a stalemate between all the sides.

Then Palmer charged the nearest man, knocking the gun from his hands. He lashed out, bloodying the man's nose. The man from the coastguard fell back and landed on his rear, looking shocked. Palmer yelled at his men, ordering them to attack.

The coastguard was reluctant to fire into a charging enemy. Bodie could see it in their eyes. But, if the Diablos gained momentum here, they might get access to the guns, and that wouldn't do his team any good.

One man opened fire hesitantly. One of the Diablos twisted and fell, reducing their number. Palmer smashed another coastguard across the head, sending him sprawling, the gun skidding overboard. The Diablos were quick and were soon among the coastguard.

Bodie and his team regrouped. The Diablos had run past them, concentrating now on the coastguard, rushing between them and flinging their fists out. Men fell left and right, spattered with blood.

The Diablos were ruthless. Palmer cut through the surprised coastguard like a machete through the forest, felling as many opponents as he could. It was up to Bodie and his team now to save the shocked coastguard.

Bodie saw the captain still aboard his ship. He was yelling into the radio, probably summoning reinforcements. But that wouldn't help him now, as his men were fully involved in an all-or-nothing fist fight.

Bodie grabbed a Diablo from behind, yanked him off a man and spun him around before delivering a blow that would shatter teeth. The man yelled out and fell and tried to grab hold of Bodie as he went down. Bodie staggered too, but managed to fling the man away. He moved on to the next opponent.

Cassidy delivered a kidney punch to her opponent and then another. He jerked and weakened and pulled away from the coastguard he'd been beating on. The coastguard raised his weapon, training it between the Diablo and Cassidy.

'Don't move!'

Bodie saw it was hopeless. The coastguard simply couldn't be certain who their enemy was. He took another Diablo down and then suddenly found himself facing Palmer.

'You!' the man cried. 'I've been waiting for this.'

Bodie grabbed a bottle from a nearby table that was surprisingly still intact. The bottle was empty. He swiped it across Palmer's face, but the man evaded the attack. The bottle flew past ineffectually. Palmer delivered two swift blows to Bodie's ribs, but then Bodie brought the bottle back on its return swing, shattering it across the man's head.

Palmer sank to his knees. Bodie stepped back and prepared to knock him out, but at that moment he was sideswiped by another Diablo and staggered to the left, away from Palmer.

It was a total brawl. The guns were largely ineffectual, being ignored by the Diablos who, essentially now, were unarmed, having lost their knives. The men from the coastguard wouldn't fire on unarmed men, and all they could do was threaten.

And get pushed back along the deck.

The Diablos showed no mercy. They beat the men from the coastguard hard and tried to throw them from the boat. Their captain screamed into his radio as the pilot of the ship continued to keep it close.

Bodie and his team continued to assault the Diablos. Palmer got back to his feet, pushed in a different direction. The fight continued, sprawling around the deck. Another coastguard raised his weapon and threatened to open fire. A Diablo threw something hard at him, the object connecting with the man's forehead and knocked him over. Another gun went flying into the sea.

And now, Bodie saw, some of the Diablos were rushing over to the coastguard ship as if they could commandeer it. He saw two men set upon as they tried to defend the ship, one of them immediately knocked to the ground and the other fumbling for his weapon.

The battle had now extended to all three vessels. Bodie knew the only way to end it was to defeat all the Diablos. Palmer especially kept rallying them with shouted commands.

He whirled, seeking an opponent. One man looked good – he was currently beating down on a fallen coastguard, bloodying the man's face. Bodie rushed over, kicked the man in the ribs and then watched him struggle to stand. He lashed out straight away, aiming for the more vulnerable areas and rendering the man senseless. The problem was – they kept debilitating the enemy but, after a while, they recovered and came back to the fight. What they really needed was handcuffs.

He turned to one of the coastguards. 'Do you have any restraints?'

The man nodded, reached into a pocket, and brought out a handful of flexi cuffs. Bodie grabbed them, then turned to cuff the man he'd just incapacitated. That was one definitely out of the action.

He looked up. His team was spread out again, having lost their momentum. He threw Cassidy and Yasmine some cuffs and looked for someone else to fight.

A knife whistled past so close to his face that he felt its breath of wind. He flinched away. The knife clattered to the deck close by, and he looked around. The thrower was already engaged with another opponent, one of the coastguard.

It was then he heard another noise, rising over the tumult. It was deep and thunderous, and when he looked up, he saw its source immediately. A large helicopter with the word "Coastguard" emblazoned across its body was approaching from the east. It was powering in low, barely skimming the waves, and there was at least one man gazing out of its open doors.

Bodie wondered if it was bringing reinforcements. More likely, it was part of the rescue team and wouldn't have known what to expect. It came closer now and then started hovering above the coastguard ship. Its rotors tore at the air as it wobbled in the sky, its wash causing the waves to churn.

Bodie saw the pilot yelling into his radio as he saw what was happening below. One of the men leaning out of the doors shouted to someone. The other rose and then sat down again. It looked as if they did not know what to do.

Bodie waved at them, trying to ward them off. They surely couldn't help this situation. The helicopter drifted closer, as if the men aboard were preparing to rappel down into the fight. Bodie waved even more frantically.

But he wasn't out of the fight. Another man attacked him, hitting him bodily across the chest. Bodie staggered back against the boat's rail, almost overbalancing but managing to save himself. With the sound of the roaring chopper in his ears, he stepped forward to meet the man's next attack, bore the expected blows and came back with some harmful ones of his own. It took him about two minutes to get the guy in cuffs.

By then, the helicopter was drifting dangerously close to Bodie's vessel, its left skid now hanging over the deck. The men aboard were donning some kind of harness and it did appear as if they were about to join forces with their colleagues.

'No,' Bodie yelled, waving again, attention off the melee once more. 'You need to get more help!'

Above the noise of the rotors nobody was going to hear him. The helicopter drifted through the air, getting closer, the skids now just a few feet above Bodie's head. He was surrounded by tumult, by crazy conflict.

And then, a deafening shout did cut through the chaos. Bodie span in place to see Palmer standing alone on the deck.

In his right hand he held a gun.

He trained it on the helicopter and fired, clearly a warning shot, as the bullet slammed through the air above the chopper. The pilot stared at him, face drawn in a rictus of fear, the radio in his right hand temporarily forgotten.

'Bring it lower,' Palmer yelled.

CHAPTER THIRTY SIX

Bodie had no idea what Palmer was doing, but he couldn't let it stand. Palmer clearly had the chopper pilot in his sights, and the man was gently lowering the craft until it almost touched the deck. There wasn't enough room for it – nowhere near – but it could hover just above the rails. All around, men and women darted out of the way to avoid the wash, the fighting temporarily forgotten.

Palmer eased his way past several of his own men. 'I'm getting the hell out of here,' he suddenly cried and started running. His own men gaped and then started after him, hoping to join. Palmer ran and then leaped for the nearest skid, pocketing the weapon for now. He reached it and climbed on, then looked up.

Bodie couldn't let it stand. He raced after the fleeing men. From the other side he saw Cassidy doing the same, tripping men as she went. Bodie did the same, reaching one runner and kicking at his legs so that he went sprawling. He gained on another, grabbed hold of his jacket and jerked him to the side so that he crashed into the rail of the boat. There was one more ahead. Bodie leapt on him with a leading elbow, smashing him to the deck, and then he was clear all the way to Palmer.

The Diablo leader was already climbing up into the chopper. Bodie reached it and jumped on beside him, landing hard and clinging onto the rail above. Palmer gave him a nasty look.

'Get the hell away from me. I'll shoot you in the stomach and throw you into the sea.'

'Not today, you won't. And you're going nowhere.'

Bodie struck out with one hand, smacking Palmer in the face. The man hit back, and standing there on the skids of the chopper, they traded blows. The aircraft trembled and shook and drifted in the air as the pilot compensated for the weight. A stiff wind tore at them and sleet lanced in from the west. Bodie clung tight to a rail and lashed out, trying to knock Palmer from his perch.

The two men battled. The chopper swung in the air. Around the deck, Cassidy and the rest of the relic hunters were taking advantage of the confusion and trying to debilitate and cuff the remaining Diablos. The coastguard men were trying to return to a semblance of order.

Bodie maintained a tight grip on the rail and lunged at Palmer's throat. The other man swayed away, then came in with a harsh slicing punch that, if it had connected, might have broken Bodie's jaw. Bodie kept him busy enough so that he could not draw his weapon. Above, the coastguard men were looking down, nonplussed.

Palmer yelled at the pilot to take the bird up. The man did nothing at first, seeing that the main threat had, for now, been negated. Bodie kicked Palmer in the knee, making his left leg buckle.

Palmer growled. He looked up, down, and tried

to make a decision. Finally, he let Bodie strike him twice in the throat and pulled out the gun. He was gargling, unable to breathe, but the barrel was trained on Bodie.

He tried to say something, couldn't speak. His eyes were glazed, but he could still pull a trigger. He fired point blank.

Bodie, expecting it, dropped off the skid and hit the deck. The bullet flew an inch over his head. He scrambled underneath the hovering chopper so that Palmer couldn't see him.

With Bodie's threat gone, Palmer climbed up the rest of the way into the cabin. Bodie still wasn't going to let him get away. He darted out from under the craft, leapt up to the skid and then chased after the man. Palmer didn't even notice his approach, and none of his men, left behind, warned him.

Bodie grabbed hold of Palmer from behind, pulled him backwards. The man let out a squawk of surprise and then angry resignation registered on his face. He snapped a hand into his jacket, reaching for the gun.

But the weapon was his downfall.

Bodie had been expecting it, knew he had Palmer's reaction time in which to act. He also knew Palmer's throat was already bruised and weakened. He threw three heavy, crunching punches into it now, saw the agony suddenly light up the man's face.

Palmer's hands flew to his throat. Bodie's own hands darted at the man's jacket and plucked out the handgun, fast as a lighting strike, a trick remembered from long ago when he was a thief. The abrupt turnaround made the cabin crew gasp.

Bodie pressed the muzzle of the gun against Palmer's cheek.

'Sit down,' he said.

When Palmer complied, Bodie leaned forward with the last of his plastic cuffs. At that instant, Palmer shot upright, barging Bodie out of the way. He jumped on top of Bodie, reaching for the gun.

Bodie kept it between his body and the floor. He saw the sizeable gap of the doorway looming behind Palmer, tucked both his feet into Palmer's stomach, and then thrust out. Palmer let out a yelp as he was suddenly propelled backwards far faster than he could handle, now backpedalling towards the open door.

With no way of stopping, he fell out of the door and flew through the air, crashing down on to the boat's deck below. When Bodie crawled over to the door and looked down, he saw Palmer had landed on his neck. The man lay unmoving, his head at an unnatural angle. Bodie winced.

'Had to hurt,' he said.

All around the deck, the Diablos were unmoving. Even before Palmer fell to his death, the fight had gone out of them. The coastguards and relic hunters moved among them, cuffing their hands behind their backs.

Bodie leaned back in to the helicopter, heaving a sigh of relief. Soon, one of the men aboard tapped him on the shoulder and pointed below.

'The captain wants to see you.'

Bodie nodded and forced himself to rise. He was aching, bruised and cut and wanted about a week of sleep. Nevertheless, he climbed out of the chopper, grabbed the skid again, and eased himself back down to the deck of the boat. A man with a large moustache and wearing glasses faced him.

'What the hell is going on here? Are you the one who phoned it in?'

'Yeah, that's me,' Bodie said. 'Let me explain.'

CHAPTER THIRTY SEVEN

Days later, and the team could spend some time by themselves away from the burden of interrogation. They had been fully cleared of all crimes and had explained in detail all the information concerning Gustave Auch. They had also given the authorities the exact position of the Lady Royal and a rundown of its potential treasure.

'That official,' Lucie said. 'When I told him the worth of the treasure, you should have seen his eyebrows shoot up.' She laughed.

The team was sitting in an upscale hotel suite, seated on the three sofas that made up the centre of the room. The tall windows looked out onto Hyde Park and offered a fine vista of that area of London and all the people passing below. It was the first time the team had relaxed in days.

'I'm so grateful,' Reilly told them all, holding a cup of coffee in one hand. 'That we achieved exactly what we set out to do. The Diablos won't be looking for me anymore.'

The entire crew had been captured and remanded in custody. They weren't talking, but the coastguard had plenty of witnesses and the captain of their boat and the extra divers were only too happy to help to avoid prosecution. The Diablos wouldn't be smelling clean air any time soon.

Reilly was beside himself. 'This entire mission has been an immense success,' he said. 'I'm finally free and it's a huge weight lifted off my shoulders. Thank you all.'

Cassidy leaned forward and touched his arm. 'Hey,' she said. 'You know you're one of us now. You're a goddamn relic hunter, and that means something.'

'We don't know wat they'll do from prison,' Reilly admitted. 'And the big boss wasn't in the mix, but I'm sure they'll have plenty of other problems to take care of now with a good chunk of their team gone.'

'Plenty,' Yasmine said.

'Are we happy we handed over the treasure?' Bodie asked, teasingly. He already knew the answer.

Lucie spoke first, as he'd known she would. 'Not in the least,' she said. 'But I guess we had no choice in the end. It helped keep us out of jail.'

'I would have liked to pursue that gold and silver,' Jemma said. 'The jewels. To help bring it all to the surface. But they don't want our help.' She pouted.

'But we *will* get credited for the find,' Bodie said. 'In certain circles. And that's good for our reputation.'

'Doesn't mean anything if we don't take advantage of it,' Cassidy said, and Bodie knew exactly what she meant. He lifted a coffee cup to his lips and took a sip.

'Look,' he said. 'There's been a lot of talk about the future of this team and I'm sorry, I've been a little distracted,' he gave Heidi a smile which made the others laugh. 'But there's something big to consider.'

Jemma popped some gum in her mouth and started to chew. 'I'll say,' she said. 'How about our future?'

Cassidy nodded. 'We all have money now,' she said. 'We could all go our own way, find honest jobs. But what the hell is one of those? I've never been honest in my life.'

More laughter. Bodie nodded at her. 'We're not your normal workers,' he said. 'Never have been, and I also don't think I could do a normal job. The money we have won't last forever, so what the hell are we gonna do?'

'If we're apart, we're weaker,' Heidi said. 'Remember on the boat? When we all fought together, we kicked their asses. When we drifted apart, it fell, well...apart.'

'The same goes for our missions in general,' Jemma said insistently. 'We work well as a team. Together.'

Bodie sat forward, resting his cup on the glass table between them. 'If we're sticking together,' he said. 'There's only one thing we can do.'

Jemma and Cassidy, his oldest friends, looked at each other expectantly. 'Which is?'

Bodie nodded at Heidi as if agreeing with something she'd said. 'We have actually discussed this at length,' he said. 'And I want to discuss it now, especially with you two.' He nodded at Cassidy and Jemma. 'Since you've been around the longest. But how about this – we form a proper genuine company? We become legit — a team of relic hunters with a great reputation. We offer our services to the world. How about it?'

'Do we have enough contacts to make it work?' Yasmine asked.

'More than you'd think,' Bodie said. 'And we can lean on them all once we get started. The jobs don't have to be huge to begin with. And our fees can't be too over the top. At least at first,' he added. 'I mean, there are always relics to be found.'

'I like it,' Cassidy said immediately and Jemma nodded along. 'Whoever hires us, they're in for a ride.'

'But let's try to keep the danger levels to a minimum in the future,' Lucie said dryly. 'We were lucky to all come out of that last battle in one piece.'

'Can't promise you that,' Bodie said, reminded of his aching limbs and ribs. 'But we never go chasing danger. It kind of starts chasing us.'

Cassidy, the only one of them with a cold beer, lifted her bottle up in salute. 'To us,' she said. 'To the relic hunters.'

'To the future,' Jemma said.

'To the new venture,' Heidi held her cup up.

Bodie eased back, smiled at his team, and drank. It was going to be a very good next few months.

THE END

Thanks for reading the latest instalment of the Relic Hunters saga. I really hope you enjoyed the ride with Bodie and co. Again, it was fun to write and I'm looking forward to taking the team on some new, fresh adventures in the future.

Next up, we're looking at a brand new Joe Mason in January and then a new Matt Drake shortly after. I'm really looking forward to seeing what I can do with the Drake team in the future. As always, if you enjoyed this book, please leave a review or a rating on Amazon. Thank you!

If you enjoyed this book, please leave a review or a rating.

The Maestro's Treasure

Other Books by David Leadbeater:

Blood Requiem

The Matt Drake Series
A constantly evolving, action-packed romp based in the escapist action-adventure genre:

The Bones of Odin (Matt Drake #1)
The Blood King Conspiracy (Matt Drake #2)
The Gates of Hell (Matt Drake 3)
The Tomb of the Gods (Matt Drake #4)
Brothers in Arms (Matt Drake #5)
The Swords of Babylon (Matt Drake #6)
Blood Vengeance (Matt Drake #7)
Last Man Standing (Matt Drake #8)
The Plagues of Pandora (Matt Drake #9)
The Lost Kingdom (Matt Drake #10)
The Ghost Ships of Arizona (Matt Drake #11)
The Last Bazaar (Matt Drake #12)
The Edge of Armageddon (Matt Drake #13)
The Treasures of Saint Germain (Matt Drake #14)
Inca Kings (Matt Drake #15)
The Four Corners of the Earth (Matt Drake #16)
The Seven Seals of Egypt (Matt Drake #17)
Weapons of the Gods (Matt Drake #18)
The Blood King Legacy (Matt Drake #19)
Devil's Island (Matt Drake #20)
The Fabergé Heist (Matt Drake #21)
Four Sacred Treasures (Matt Drake #22)

The Sea Rats (Matt Drake #23)
Blood King Takedown (Matt Drake #24)
Devil's Junction (Matt Drake #25)
Voodoo soldiers (Matt Drake #26)
The Carnival of Curiosities (Matt Drake #27)
Theatre of War (Matt Drake #28)
Shattered Spear (Matt Drake #29)
Ghost Squadron (Matt Drake #30)
A Cold Day in Hell (Matt Drake #31)
The Winged Dagger (Matt Drake #32)
Two Minutes to Midnight (Matt Drake #33)
The Devil's Reaper (Matt Drake#34)
The Dark Tsar (Matt Drake #35)

The Alicia Myles Series
Aztec Gold (Alicia Myles #1)
Crusader's Gold (Alicia Myles #2)
Caribbean Gold (Alicia Myles #3)
Chasing Gold (Alicia Myles #4)
Galleon's Gold (Alicia Myles #5)
Hawaiian Gold (Alicia Myles #6)

The Torsten Dahl Thriller Series
Stand Your Ground (Dahl Thriller #1)

The Relic Hunters Series
The Relic Hunters (Relic Hunters #1)
The Atlantis Cipher (Relic Hunters #2)
The Amber Secret (Relic Hunters #3)
The Hostage Diamond (Relic Hunters #4)

The Rocks of Albion (Relic Hunters #5)
The Illuminati Sanctum (Relic Hunters #6)
The Illuminati Endgame (Relic Hunters #7)
The Atlantis Heist (Relic Hunters #8)
The City of a Thousand Ghosts (Relic Hunters #9)
Hierarchy of Madness (Relic Hunters #10)

The Joe Mason Series
The Vatican Secret (Joe Mason #1)
The Demon Code (Joe Mason #2)
The Midnight Conspiracy (Joe Mason #3)
The Babylon Plot (Joe Mason #4)
The Traitor's Gold (Joe Mason #5)
The Angel Deception (Joe Mason #6)

The Rogue Series
Rogue (Book One)

The Disavowed Series:
The Razor's Edge (Disavowed #1)
In Harm's Way (Disavowed #2)
Threat Level: Red (Disavowed #3)

The Chosen Few Series
Chosen (The Chosen Trilogy #1)
Guardians (The Chosen Trilogy #2)
Heroes (The Chosen Trilogy #3)

Short Stories

Walking with Ghosts (A short story)
A Whispering of Ghosts (A short story)

All genuine comments are very welcome at:

davidleadbeater2011@hotmail.co.uk

Twitter: @dleadbeater2011

Visit David's website for the latest news and information:
davidleadbeater.com

Printed in Great Britain
by Amazon